STEAMTOWN CHRONICLES 1: THE DARK MARKET

RJ CASTIGLIONE

RJ CASTIGLIONE BOOKS

TABLE OF CONTENTS

Chapter 1   1
Chapter 2   17
Chapter 3   27
Chapter 4   41
Chapter 5   55
Chapter 6   69
Chapter 7   81
Chapter 8   91
Chapter 9   111

About the Author   123
Also by RJ Castiglione   125

1
———

I was focusing fervently on the vibrating rune on my workbench when a jingle announced the arrival of a new customer in the front of the store. I clenched my jaw tightly, frustrated that someone interrupted the most intricate part of forming an enchanting rune.

"Delmen, you there?" a voice called from the front. The trembling glyph on the table beckoned me. I knew if I left it now, it would mean wasting an hour of work and all the materials that went into forming a glyph ready to sell.

"Give me a minute!" I called out to the potential customer. My voice sounded muffled in my tiny workroom, like someone yelling in a buried coffin. I squinted at the glyph, focusing on the intricate etching needed to complete the job.

Just one more infusion, I thought, but as I collected a small amount of mana into my hammer and prepared to etch in the last symbol for an *Apprentice Stoneskin* enchantment, a loud crash from the front distracted me. My chisel slipped, scratching a deep groove across the delicate gemstone. The opal began to quiver within the vice securing it to the table as magic leaked out, sending a cascade of rainbow lights across my workroom until the stone split.

I held my head low in resignation at the spent product broken in front of me. It would have sold for enough guilders to pay rent for the next month and was the most advanced enchantment I was allowed to create.

"I don't have a minute! Get your ass out here before I report you for mandate violation!"

I recognized the voice now. It belonged to Dairadin, the general shopkeeper from Paladin's Close, a dozen alleys down. Sliding off my stool, I trudged across the room and into the front.

"Damn you, Dairadin! You made me ruin a perfectly good opal!"

I was met by an exhausted fellow dwarf lugging a sack of goods ready to sell. "Not my fault," he said as he struggled to lift a drooping half of the bag onto the counter. "If you don't want your enchants ruined, you could request a clerk to man the storefront."

"You know how long that takes? And how much clerks cost? No thanks." Stepping on my footstool to get a better look, I hesitated to open the bag, knowing Dairadin well. He wasn't interested in trading for enchantments. His Mandate dictated he only sell general goods to travelers, yet he was allowed to sell anything he purchased to any other vendor he desired. For some unknown reason, he went out of his way to unload his junk on me. Still, his wares provided me ample weapons and armor to disenchant for crafting materials, only today's goods proved lackluster.

"What's this? Why even bring these here?" I asked him as I pulled out a mound of nonsense ranging from herbs to raw meat to leather skins to the lowest level weapons possible, all but one unenchanted. "What do you expect me to do with these?"

"What do I expect?" the older dwarf asked me. "I expect you to act like a vendor and buy them from me like your mandates demand!"

I rolled my eyes at him as he pulled out a small book and waved it in the air. I had a matching book myself, tailored to me, issued by Governor Law before I was assigned my profession, store, and lodgings. My book currently served as a tea coaster to prevent water rings from dotting up my countertop, but I remembered the rules well.

Steamtown Mandates for Common Magical Shopkeeper:

1. Under no circumstances should citizens leave Steamtown. Doing so can result in arrest and reassignment to common labor.

2. All shopkeepers will maintain strict hours. Shops should be opened from sunrise to sunset. Upon closing, shops should be locked with a master level lock.

3. All shopkeepers must sell goods specific only to the shop in question. Other purchased products must be recycled immediately. General goods vendors are exempted and may sell goods to any other vendors.

4. All shopkeepers will be assigned a single-room residence in their associated close, penned in below:

Name: Delmen MacDougall

Location: Crafter's Close, level 1, apartment 2

Shop Location: Crafter's Close, level 1, ground floor

Shop Mandate: Novice and Apprentice enchantments

5. When not at home, the residence is to be locked by a novice level lock.

6. Shopkeepers are instructed to remain at their current level in all skills and professions. Under no circumstances should a vendor attempt to increase their profession level. Punishable by reassignment.

7. Shopkeepers must purchase all goods offered to them at common market value, no more, no less. Any attempt to provide different prices will result in a fine equal to six month's wages.

8. Citizens must return home by midnight. Anyone caught violating curfew will be subject to a fine of one month's wages.

9. All citizens are subject to random inspections by guards.

Anyone found breaking these mandates will be subject to reassignment. Multiple violations can result in assignment to various punitive locations.

10. The Great Mandate is in effect despite assignment. Under no circumstances should a citizen attack a traveler, even in self-defense. Anyone killed by a traveler will be resurrected within two days and be rewarded with seventy-two-hour passive immunity. Anyone caught attacking a traveler will be arrested and reassigned permanently to Steamtown Stockades.

I searched through the sack, sorting through an ever-shrinking coin pouch, handing over 1 guilder and 78 pieces to the angry dwarf. He claimed the coins and stomped out of the shop, knocking over a small stand of tools along the way.

Once the door shut, I tucked my black hair behind my ears and scanned the purchased goods. While some vendors like Dairadin wouldn't dare violate their mandates, many of us couldn't afford not to. Sure, I wouldn't advance my level in any professions or skills, but I wouldn't recycle a good hunk of meat and some herbs that would make for an excellent supper. I claimed one of the tanned animal skins, wrapped up my now-bought dinner, and tucked it under the counter.

The rest of the nonsense littering my counter proved useless. I couldn't sell it again. Only general store owners were allowed to sell to other vendors. I recycled the lot of them by stuffing each item into my inventory and then dragging them to the destroy bin to be reallocated elsewhere. All that remained was the common-quality dagger ready to be disenchanted.

Hoping I wouldn't get another customer for the day, I grabbed the dagger, retreated into the back of the shop, and got to work at my enchanting table, opposite my crafter's workbench. With a bucket of shrine water and a bowl of glow dust, I formed a paste to coat the dagger, leaving it for the hours it would take to consume the blade down to the materials embedded within, either a gemstone to be used for future glyphs or, most likely, more dust to be used for enchanting and disenchanting work.

As I cleaned up, the cathedral bells rang, signaling the end of the workday. I eagerly pocketed my dinner and closed up shop before anyone interrupted me. Guards were especially tough on vendors who kept their stores open after hours. I didn't need another fine after forking over so much coin to Dairadin.

Stepping outside for the first time that day, I felt short of breath and dizzy. Of all the towns and villages of Eto, the only world I knew, Steamtown was the dirtiest. Or so I assumed. The air was so thick with smog from the many factories and coal plants you could taste it, and I didn't like air I could taste. I much preferred air I could breathe. Careful to lock my door, I thought about going upstairs and starting dinner. I had a few hours to spare and could wait for some of the other vendors to close up and see where they were heading. Deciding to take a moment to see if anything interesting was happening, I leaned against the coal-stained stones of my shop's outer wall as other citizens and travelers strode by, a hodgepodge of humans, elves, gnomes, dwarves like myself, and other more uncommon races.

Staring at the shop opposite the road, I wondered what Meridia was up to and if I was in any state to go for a drink if she invited me. My cheeks were usually stained with soot, polished by smudges of glow dust. My shoulder-length hair was matted and twisted, most of it tied up in a knot behind my head. The makings of a stubble suggested I was in need of a clean shave, something most dwarves didn't care to do. Dairadin, a dwarf through and through, preferred to let his beard grow long and curly, most likely to hide his ugly mug, but Meridia, an elf, once told me my face was too young and handsome to hide behind a long beard and thick mustache, so I kept everything tidy.

I continued to peer into her shop window. Her store, Goldneedle's Fabrics, was one of my favorite places to be in Crafter's Close outside of my workroom. Not only was she a dear friend, but her beauty and the scent of her blended perfume chased away the fetid miasma that lingered over the entire market district. In my opinion, her shop was one of the best smelling places in the city, second only to the Royal Gardens dividing the common districts from the High Mile, a stretch of upper-class shops, brownstones, estates, and the Governor's mansion lining the street up to the Queen's Palace.

I spotted Meridia leaving her store and waved to her, but she didn't see me. Instead, a man walked up to her, a traveler, and the two left arm in arm, away toward the center of town. I thought about catching up with her but hesitated.

A cry of "gardyloo" came from above me. The splash of bodily waste on the ground of the close pushed me back into the wall.

"Laundry it is," I muttered to myself as I tip-toed around the puddle of a spent chamber pot. Peering down the close, I knew conditions lower down weren't as good as they were at the street level. The steep, narrow alley was slick with waste, few of us being lucky enough to have indoor toilets. I was the most fortunate, or so I liked to think, having a shop and resi-dence on the highest level of the close, and counted myself blessed I wasn't assigned to a home at the bottom with hundreds of other residents tossing their waste out to collect in a rank puddle until the next rain washed it away.

"Gardyloo!" another citizen shouted from deeper in the close.

I rushed inside before I got splashed again and wound my way up the spiral staircase to the second story and my flat, just above my shop. I would have fumbled with the keyring to unlock the door but found it propped open with some broken lockpicks littering the ground. I peered inside looking for any sign of a traveler, hoping they weren't still inside rummaging through my things.

I was in luck, though. Nothing was out of sorts, and my tiny apartment was empty. It looked more like a case of a traveler trying to increase their lockpicking or sneaking skills. I cursed the fact that travelers were allowed to level when we weren't.

Months prior, when I walked in on a traveler mid-burgle only to be killed, I made a point to be more careful and hid any valuables in a jewelry chest under the floorboards where they wouldn't be discovered. Carefully propping up the loose board, I found the box and its contents intact.

I closed the door and triggered the four magelight glyphs I had embedded into the wall of my tiny apartment, gleeful that I didn't have to use rush or tallow lights like some of my poorer neighbors. I got to work on the bit of meat and herbs I saved from downstairs. Within minutes, the wretched stench of the close was chased away by the smell of sizzling steak and pungent herbs.

Once dinner was consumed, and the smell of the meal faded, I opened my door again to cool the apartment down. Still before midnight, I stepped out onto the little walkway in time to spot a traveler across the alley and a few doors down, crouched outside a neighbor's flat. He worked a lockpick on the door.

Within a few seconds of my spotting him, a blinking eye above his head illuminated and opened. He pocketed the lockpick, frustrated, and looked around until he saw me.

"Fucking NPC!"

I didn't know what an NPC was, but travelers often called us citizens by that name. They used it in an unflattering way, meant to insult and belittle us. Despite Steamtown being our home, they reigned supreme, and could even walk up to the queen, fully armed, without anyone challenging them.

I froze in place, unsure of what to do, and glanced at my nameplate glowing a soft blue above my head. <<*Delmen MacDougall -- LVL 9*>>. Although too far away to read, the traveler's nameplate shined green. I observed it, hoping it wouldn't change to red, a sign the traveler was about to attack me.

I hated dying. Everything about it was uncomfortable. The pain of death was intolerable. Spending time in self-aware oblivion until resurrecting at the Cathedral's graveyard was hardly a vacation. It meant days away from the shop and made paying rent difficult. So when the traveler pulled out a rifle, I backed up slowly into my flat, closed and locked the door. I crouched against it with my back pressed into the rough wood for good measure, hoping the angry traveler ignored me and went on his way.

Staying like that until I fell asleep, I woke the next morning with a crick in my neck and the feeling of an iron rod in my back, as though I'd never move again. With a great deal of effort, I lurched upward and came to with enough time to hear the morning bell ring. I had thirty minutes before I had to open the shop. I made my way downstairs to avoid the shower of morning chamber pots.

On a typical morning, opening the shop was a non-event. One day blended into the next, day after day after day with dozens of other shopkeepers opening their stores at the same time, keys turned and doors squeaking open before the final morning bell chimed.

Only this morning, I spotted Meridia sitting on the stoop outside her store wearing the same hand-made dress she wore the night before, a frilly sequence of jade green fabric and embroidered beads. Her hat and shawl were nowhere in sight, and she looked worn, tired, and sad.

I watched a dozen citizens walk by her, ignoring her so

they could get to their shops and avoid guards threatening them with fines for mandate violations. I didn't care, though. Meridia was my friend, and she looked like she needed to talk. I finished unlocking my door, flipped my store sign to open, and crossed the street, narrowly dodging a few carts already on their way out of town. I sat next to her, wondering if I should speak first or if she would say something. We sat in silence for a few moments while she dried her puffy cheeks with a pure white handkerchief.

I gave up on the silence first. "Are you all right?"

She huffed and brushed some dirt off her dress, but still didn't speak.

"I guess your evening with the traveler last night didn't go so well?"

"How did you know?" she asked.

"What else could it be? You're still wearing the same dress as yesterday. That's so unlike you."

She giggled a little, then curled her hand into a fist, wrinkling her handkerchief. I noticed her coin purse in her other hand. It looked empty. "I just don't get it. Why are travelers so cruel? He invited me out to dinner and next thing I knew, he led me down Garden Close next to the cathedral and robbed me blind! Before I knew what he was doing, all my money, my hat, my shawl, and my dagger were gone, and so was he! I feel like such a silly, little girl!"

She tossed her empty coin purse on the ground before burying her face in her hands. I didn't know what to do or say. She was foolish for trusting travelers, many of whom seemed more interested in taking everything we had. They would sooner kill us than treat us as equals. But she was also the victim in this. She was blameless.

I hesitated for a second before wrapping my arm around her shoulder. I felt silly, not because Meridia and I had never touched before, but because my thick, dwarf arm seemed far too burly for her slender figure, like a bear hugging a swan.

"It's okay," I said to her in a firm, but gentle tone. "Everything will be okay."

She shrugged my arm off her shoulder. "No, it won't! My rent is due tomorrow. I have no way to make the payment on time."

"Is there anything I can do?" I asked. I felt my coin pouch tied to my belt, half-full, and looked at my ratty work clothes. "Perhaps I can buy a nice outfit from you? Something I can wear out at night."

"That's sweet of you, Delmen, but you're in no position to buy my wares. I saw how Dairadin fleeced you yesterday. I'll figure something out."

"Do you think you'll lose the store?" I asked her. I felt selfish, suddenly, worrying more about Meridia going away rather than what might happen to her. She was one of the few bright spots in my life. I worried about how lonely I would feel not seeing her every day. She was, without a doubt, my only friend, as life in Steamtown didn't leave much room for lasting friendships.

"I have enough for the store, but not enough for the flat, and I'd hate having to move into the common house or deeper into the close. You understand how things are. Once you lose your flat, reassignment isn't far behind."

"I honestly don't think that'll happen to you," I said. "You're too clever."

She smiled. Her slender shoulders relaxed a bit as she dabbed more tears from her cheeks. She unexpectedly blew her nose into the handkerchief before putting it away. "That's so sweet of you to say, Delmen. You've always been such a good friend to me."

I cringed at the way she emphasized "friend." I wanted to tell her that I desired more than friendship, that I would sleep on the floor and let her have my bed if it kept her close, but before I could say anything, I spotted trouble coming up the road — a group of guards in red tabards doing their morning rounds.

"Enforcers," I muttered. "You'd better go inside. Want to go out after work? My treat."

She smiled and kissed me on the cheek. I felt heat rushing to my face, and hoped I didn't blush too much.

"You're always so good to me. Thank you," she said before she rushed inside, not giving me an answer.

I, too, hurried to my shop, albeit with less grace than Meridia, my oversized feet and clunky boots tripping me up as I jogged.

I breathed a sigh of relief when I got inside and the guards, oblivious to our mandate violation, pressed on. When I turned my attention away from the door, though, something seemed off. Usually, I was met by the white flicker of my magelight glyphs, only they were dark and cold, as though all magic had been drained from them. Behind the tattered curtain leading to my workroom, a blue aura pulsed, sending ripples of light cascading across the floor.

I hesitated, not sure what might cause the light, but remembered the dagger disenchantment I had started the night before. With my work hammer in hand, I crept across the room, mindful not to trip over the stand Dairadin knocked down, and entered my workshop.

The light was intense, more intense than anything I had seen before. Shielding my eyes, I discarded my hammer and moved to the enchanting table. It took a moment for my vision to adjust to the brightness, but when it did, I gasped. Atop the table, coated in a fine layer of powdery glow dust, a divine crystal waited to be claimed.

As I reached out to pick it up, I felt a tingling in my fingers as some of my innate mana was sucked away to fill the gemstone. As it absorbed my magic, it pulsed and vibrated. When I gripped the stone in my strong hands, made powerful by years of manual labor, I felt a comfortable warmth move up my arm, as though the gemstone wanted to be a part of me.

I had never seen anything like it, though I knew what it was: an epic-quality gem used for the creation of self-charging Grandmaster weapon enchantments, well above the mandated level I could craft.

It made me nervous, and paranoid. I grabbed a nearby rag and wrapped up the gem to diffuse the light pouring into my storefront, afraid a guard would walk by and catch me red-handed.

The punishment for even considering leveling crafting skills was instant reassignment, often to the mines outside the city, where folks were forced to sleep on the ground and lived off stale bread they earned only after reaching their daily quota, or so I'd heard.

I should recycle this, I thought. But I didn't want to. The gem was precious enough that, even if sold in its raw form, the proceeds could cover my shop rent for half a year. An enchantment produced by it could pay for my current status for two years, at least.

I still couldn't believe such a rudimentary weapon yielded an epic gemstone. It was a shame I couldn't use it. I certainly couldn't risk selling it. If other general store owners were like Dairadin, they would report me immediately for mandate violation, and I would be ruined. Most couldn't afford to buy it anyway.

I did the only logical thing. I put the gem into my inventory where it would be both secret and secure. There, it couldn't be stolen unless by a skilled pickpocket. It would need to remain there until I could secure it in my hidden chest upstairs.

As the day dragged on, I found myself struggling to do my job. I worried every time a customer came inside, whether it was a citizen looking to sell me their junk, or a traveler looking for enchantment materials or fully formed glyphs for their gear. Throughout the day, the number of guilders in my pouch shrank and grew, as though the pouch had a life of its own. As I tallied the total near the end of the business day, I smiled. I had earned a profit enough to make up for Dairadin's junk sale the day before.

I felt an immediate urge to close the shop and rush upstairs when the evening bells began to ring, as though the gem in my inventory weighed me down. I imagined enforcers would pass by at any moment and be able to tell that I was guilty of mandate violation just by looking at me, that the beads of sweat forming on my brow were evidence of guilt alone.

Once outside, I coughed a little. The evening fog was unusually thick. I looked up and down the street for signs of any guards but could only see fifty feet in each direction. As I turned to lock my store, I peered down Crafter's Close and couldn't see the bottom. With no guards in sight, I stood in my usual place, with my back pressed against my shop's soot-stained stone, for my chance at my evening glimpse of Meridia. I recalled promising her a meal out tonight, and the jingling of guilders in my pouch meant I could afford a standard pub meal for two.

So I waited for her as the bells chimed. Other store owners closed up shop for the night, some venturing deeper into the city, others retreating into their assigned close to go home. But Meridia showed no sign of closing. When the bells stopped, and she was officially violating her mandates, I worried. I squinted through the thick fog, attempting to see if she was there, and spotted two silhouettes outlined behind her opaque window glass, one looking like her, and the other a more hulking figure of a man.

Then I heard a crash and a scream. Not just any scream. Meridia's scream. I panicked, imagining the worst, and raged at the thought of a traveler killing her because he could. Another cry sent me into action. If I could save her from days of emptiness before she resurrected again, if I could rescue her from the pain of death, I would.

Damn the mandates! I thought as I rushed across the street, hammer in hand. I burst through the door to a scene of horror. A traveler's bright red nameplate taunted me. He was the same man from the night before come to finish fleecing her for everything she owned. A bounty tag glowed next to his name. Any guards who caught him would force him to pay 250 guilders to clear his bounty or send him to prison.

I caught my foot on her tattered coin purse and slid a little across the floor. I spotted guilders littering the ground around Meridia, who sat collapsed on the floor with a bruised and bleeding arm held up defending herself.

"Delmen, you shouldn't be here!" she cried.

"Listen to the bitch, dwarf. This doesn't concern you!" the man said. He spat on her and kicked her before turning his attention to me. I winced a bit as his foot slammed into her ribs. She writhed and heaved as she tried to catch her breath.

I locked eyes with the traveler, a human named <<*Sampson Smiter -- LVL 5*>>. When I spotted bloodstains on Meridia's beautiful carpets, I became enraged. Sampson raised his wand to cast a spell at me but he was too late. I threw my body into him and, for the first time in my entire life, blatantly disregarded my mandates to protect her.

"Delmen, no," Meridia said, trying to form words between bouts of coughing. She wouldn't stop me, though. She couldn't stop me. The two of us toppled over her and crashed into the floor with such force the entire shop trembled. Grappling on the ground, I struggled to wrest the wand from his tiny hands, but he held onto it for dear life.

"You're not supposed to attack me!" the man cried. "NPCs are always neutral!"

"I'll show you neutral!" I screamed. I was much stronger than him and was able to get to my feet, pull him up by the collar, and shove him toward the door, positioning myself between him and Meridia. She grabbed my ankle and pleaded with me to stop.

"Delmen, it's not worth it," she said. I couldn't hear her, though. All my built up frustration toward travelers culminated into a single, mighty swing of my hammer. As the man raised his wand to try to cast another spell, I swiped my hammer upwards, striking him in the chin, and sending him flying out the open doorway and into the street below. Already injured from our struggle, the impact left him a bloodied, broken corpse outside Meridia's shop, his blood pooling out of his body to stain the cobblestone under him.

I stood there for what felt like forever, blood dripping from my hammer to stain my boots. A long siren sound rang in my ears. Above me, my nameplate flickered from blue to red, back to blue, back to red, until it stuck that way and text popped up in my field of vision.

<<+1000g bounty in the city of Steamtown.>>
<< One-handed weapons rank 2.>>

My stomach lurched as I read the bounty amount, completely disregarding my skill increase. The bounty was more guilders than I made in two years. Even selling the divine crystal wouldn't get me a fraction of that amount. As I heard Meridia shuffle behind me and lift herself up, I began to panic, realizing the severity of my crime and its punishment — permanent reassignment to Steamtown Stockades.

"Oh, Delmen. What did you do?" she asked.

I turned around, still out of breath, still gasping for air from the brief struggle. What I saw hurt my heart. Meridia, still bleeding from a gash on her arm, backed away from me, too afraid to look at me. Then I heard a sharp whistle from outside and turned my head to see guards running down the street toward me.

I looked at her as tears formed in my eyes. "I don't know. I couldn't let him hurt you."

She softened a bit, and rubbed her forehead, leaving a smear of blood across it. "Run," she whispered. "Just run." So I did. Without hesitating, I turned tail and fled from the encroaching guards, first straight down Commercial Way, the main road on our side of the city, then down a random close, hoping they wouldn't chase me.

2

At the bottom of yet another unknown close, I stopped to gasp for air, nearly collapsing on the slick path multiple times. I passed first-level homes where many men, women, and children fled inside at the sight of me, afraid I was some maniac citizen on a rampage. My hammer, still coated with blood, didn't make things any easier, but I kept it held tightly in my hand, ready to defend myself should the guards pursuing me catch up.

I refused to abandon my life for one mistake, hearing horror stories of citizens reassigned to the stockades dying endlessly for the pleasure of any travelers who wanted to enter. I didn't believe the stories, of course, and considered the stockades more of a generic prison. I ran until my name-plate began to flicker again. I expected it to return to blue, but it didn't. Instead, the text hovering over my head, something everyone in Steamtown possessed, shone a bright green, like I was a traveler. The bounty text still shined clear next to it, a mark for everyone to see what I had done.

As I crept along a narrow terrace on the lake's shore at the bottom of Frederick's Close, a street unfamiliar to me, I felt it was time I hiked back up to Commercial Way. The sun had set now. It was easier for me to stick to the shadows where my nameplate was less visible. Most of the houses in this close were closed now. I could tell when creeping by the buildings that most of the apartments here spanned multiple levels, housing wealthier citizens. The close was also cleaner than mine, the ground seemingly polished to perfection rather than muddied by contents of dumped chamber pots.

I reached the top of the hill, still hidden, and peered left and right. I spotted a few citizens and some travelers who didn't notice me but saw no sign of guards in pursuit. I was close to Cathedral Plaza, only a few streets away from North Bridge and South Bridge. Across the road, I spotted the street market for Paladin's Close and Dairadin's General Store, locked for the night. I wondered for a moment if he would hide me, but I knew him well enough. He didn't care whether or not I went broke if he could unload his junk at my store. He even went out of his way to make it so, where most other general store owners had the courtesy to spread out their sales to not hurt one person too much.

He was also a stickler for the rules, a lawful citizen to an extreme, and would sooner report me than offer me refuge. No. I had to find somewhere to hide and hope my bounty faded over time. The guards were far enough away. They might not know who I was. Meridia may have kept my identity a secret.

I continued to walk down Commerce Way until I spotted the giant cathedral at the center of the plaza, a monstrosity of blackened sandstone with huge towers and spires extending upward. To some, the building was the prize of Steamtown. To me, it looked more like a prison, hardly worthy of the Five Eternals, the divine sisters who rule over Eto. I thought of my goddess, Braka, and tried to pierce my eyes through the thick smog to find her stars, the very same stars that shone high in the sky the day I was born, but I saw nothing but city lights reflecting off the clouds, interrupted only by the occasional dirigible floating over the city.

Absent the goddess's shining stars, I felt wholly alone. No person in the world could help me now. Very few would. I had nowhere to go.

"If I knew how to fly, I could steal one and escape," I muttered to myself. I didn't know how to fly, though, and escaping Steamtown wouldn't clear my bounty. I thought instantly of stories I heard from tavern bards, of the more unsavory citizens in Steamtown who supposedly managed to violate their mandates with complete abandon, who knew secret tunnels and passages where they could avoid the spine-like pattern of city streets.

I had once witnessed guards corner such a citizen, trapping him in a close, pushing him to the middle from both ends. He couldn't even climb out if he wanted to, as every close only had two staircases, one on both ends. I never saw that citizen again.

Clearing my thoughts, I focused on my next steps. My heart pounded in my chest, driven by my fear of being caught. Briefly, I considered taking sanctuary in the cathedral, but had never heard of citizens being granted a haven there. When I reached Cathedral Plaza and observed the wide-open space, I knew I couldn't cross it. Through the smog, I spotted red tabards marching toward me. I crouched and noticed, for the first time, an eyeball icon appear above my head. The eye was closed. A broad, golden ring appeared in my field of vision, extending half the length of the plaza. I had a hunch if the enforcers crossed into the ring, there was a chance they would spot me, so I ducked behind a nearby hedge outside an elegant looking house built not out of wood, like most of my tenement building, but the same type of sandstone that made up the cathedral.

My white shirt contrasted with the building's blackened stones. Digging my free hand into the ground, I scooped up some soil and smeared it over the front of my shirt, hoping it would camouflage me better. When I finished, the golden ring shrank, extending out from me only a few feet. The eye icon above me remained closed as the enforcers approached. I held my breath as they got within fifteen feet of me and stayed as still as a statue.

The eye icon opened a bit as they passed but the guards didn't seem to notice. They didn't spot me. They didn't catch my green nameplate. They didn't see my bounty.

<<Sneak rank 2>>

These new notifications I could see and the new visual effects puzzled me. At first, I thought they were visible to everyone. Now, I wasn't so sure. I didn't want to linger on it for long and abandoned the bushes once the enforcers moved out of sight. Crouching down, I skirted the perimeter of the plaza until I reached the intersection leading to North Bridge. The massive bridge spanned the glen separating Commerce Way, the city's market district, from North Slope, the city's cultural hub, home to theaters, bars, eateries, colleges, and some guild halls.

It was my best bet. If the cathedral wouldn't hide me, and if I couldn't escape the city's guarded gates, I needed to flee the market district. As I approached the bridge, my plan for safe passage fluttered away. A sudden updraft of wind typical to this part of the city blew all the smog away, providing clear visibility to the middle of the pass, where a walking patrol headed my way.

I cursed under my breath, having forgotten the bridge patrol that walked back and forth all day and night, to ward away any who might attempt to scale the cliffs from below from entering the city. I crouched again, and a golden ring filled my vision. It extended a quarter of the way across the bridge. I needed a hiding place immediately. Turning around to flee back across the square, I paused and panicked. Another group of guards entered the square, perhaps the same enforcers from before. Both groups closed in on me, oblivious to my presence. The closed eye above my head began to pulse and slowly open. I knew I would be discovered.

With nowhere else to go, I stepped back to the edge of the bridge and found a bit of worn path leading below. It disappeared into the dark glen, like an abyss waiting for me. Blind to where the trail led, I crept down. My stealth ring moved with me, reforming to the landscape until it was no longer on the bridge. The ring snaked its way over jagged outcroppings of rocks a hundred feet under me.

My foot slid, and I dropped a little until I caught myself. Looking up at the eyeball above me, I held my breath as it shot half-open. Remaining as still as ice, I waited until the eye closed before I dared to move again. I found myself on a small landing below the first of the bridge's archways, where I pressed my back against it and closed my eyes, afraid of what would happen next.

The tip-tap of soldier's boots above me sent chills down my spine. Even with my eyes closed, I could still see the menacing eyeball above me and the golden ring around me, now reduced to the size of a wagon wheel.

"Did you hear something?" I heard a woman's voice say.

I opened one eye and looked up to see an enforcer leaning over the bridge and looking down into the valley. The eye opened more, now three-quarters. I thought about retreating deeper under the arch, but no part of me could move beyond my heart pounding in my ears.

My lungs burned for want of air, but I refused to exhale, knowing even one gasp meant discovery. As a second guard joined her, the eyeball opened wider. My nameplate, invisible to them, pulsed as it started to turn from green to red.

Please, Braka, save me, I thought. The image of Braka's holy symbol, three rays of light erupting from a single star, came to mind. If the goddess intervened, I promised to tattoo the symbol on the top of my hand, so that everyone who saw it would know I serve the goddess of creation, patroness to craftsmen everywhere.

My lungs felt like they were going to burst, and my vision started to darken, when an updraft of wind blew again, this one strong enough to press me into the archway. It pushed back the guards as well, and the eye above me snapped shut.

"It was just the wind," another guard said.

I heard their footsteps move away, giving me a window enough to gasp in fresh air until my darkened vision cleared. With the guards at a safe distance, I was able to sneak further under the archway where no light could touch me, and no one could hear or see me. I sat on the sloping ground with my back pressed uncomfortably into the arch, enough to force my head down, and a wave of exhaustion washed over me.

The cathedral bell rang, signaling the evening curfew. My stomach responded with pangs of its own. I hadn't eaten in twelve hours. The combination of weariness from my escape, hunger, and worry about Meridia had me drifting in and out of a fitful sleep for the next six hours until the first sign of light glistened over the horizon and filled the glen with a golden glow. A hundred feet below me the surface of the narrow lake stretched the full length of the valley, from the cliffs outside the western castle to the open plains of the east.

As the sun rose higher, the glow on the water lessened. I realized for the first time how fetid and dirty Steamtown was. With brown water below and a nearly perpetual ash cloud suspended in the air, I knew my only correct path forward was to abandon my mandates entirely, find a way to clear my bounty, and escape Steamtown once and for all, bringing Meridia with me if I could, if she would go.

What was she doing right now? If the traveler had never attacked her, I assume she would be opening her shop, but I worried that after I left, the guards might take her in for questioning. She would miss her rent, lose her flat, and be forced to live in the Common House, a despicable facility on Pauper's Close where folks slept upright on benches, held in place only by a rope. I remembered my days in the Common House before Governor Law decided to reassign me. I hated the idea of her having to stay there and thought that if I could get back to her again, I could perhaps slip her the coin necessary to pay her lease.

The sound of a thud interrupted my thoughts, and I jolted upright, knocking my head on the archway above. Rubbing an already forming bump on my skull, I looked around for the source of the noise, hoping guards weren't climbing down the slope looking for me.

Another thud, this time below me. I looked down and realized I hadn't slept on stone. I was sitting on an exposed, wooden hatch. I stood up, careful not to slide down the slope. As I did, the hatch shot open and revealed a dark room within, completely hidden save a few rungs of a rickety ladder. Out popped a bald, green head followed by the rest of a creature, a level 13 goblin with a blue nameplate and no bounty.

The goblin stared at me, curious about my presence. "Out or in?" he asked.

"In? In where?"

"The Dark Market, of course. By the looks of you, it seems like it's the only place you should be right about now. So, out or in?"

I hesitated. I've lived in the city my entire life, and I never heard about a place called the Dark Market.

"Make up your mind, dwarf! I'm closing this entrance. I don't got all day!"

"In, definitely in," I said. The goblin tapped his foot impatiently as I did my best to crawl into the tiny hole, hardly wide enough to fit my shoulders. I felt as though the ladder would collapse on me, but as I went rung by rung into an unknown area of the city, I felt relieved, hoping it would be safe from the guards.

Before I entered, I looked up at the goblin. "What's down here?" I asked.

"For most folks, death and despair. For you, though, it beats getting caught by the guards." His raspy voice sounded gleeful, as though he enjoyed the idea of people suffering. Before I had a chance to respond, he closed the hatch shut, nearly knocking me on the head in the process.

With daylight gone completely, I forced my eyes open as wide as they would go, hoping to catch even a sliver of light. I didn't know how far down the ladder went and without an ability to see it, I hesitated to climb. Only my curiosity drove me forward, eager to find not only safety but food and a place to sleep.

I swallowed a lump in my throat and inhaled air so stale and dry it felt suffocating. Carefully lowering one foot, I found the next rung, then the next. I did this until my foot struck what I hoped was solid ground. I reached around with my arms, failing to find a wall, and inched forward carefully hoping there was no drop.

After a few minutes of shuffling around, I found a few walls, but no exit. With no light to see by, I remembered the gem in my bag and its luminescent properties. Pulling it out, I waited for my eyes to adjust, finding myself in a large chamber consisting of four nearly unbroken walls. The ladder behind me didn't lead to a hatch. Instead, it seemed fixed into solid stone, as though no exit ever existed. On the wall opposite the ladder, a small tunnel, hardly large enough for me, looked like the only way out.

After slotting my hammer in a strap on my belt, I got on my stomach and wormed my way through the tunnel, catching my broad shoulders on the sides of it. A few times I feared I was stuck, but after exhaling as much as possible, I managed to squeeze through the entire length of sloping tunnel further into the hidden underground. Once through, the tube behind me sealed shut, turning, like the entrance, to smooth stone. Ahead of me, a tunnel spiraled into the ground as though a massive corkscrew carved it.

Now able to stand, I traced my hand along the wall as I walked, careful to peer around every bend for signs of life. A few minutes later, the spiral ended. The narrow tunnel fanned out into an underground chamber illuminated by hundreds of magelight glyphs. I didn't know what to expect, but what I witnessed left me speechless. The cavern defied reason. Lining the walls, dozens of stalls sold all sorts of goods, from food to enchantments to weapons and armor to potions. Hundreds of citizens meandered from one vendor to the next, perusing stall owner's wares.

They all stopped what they were doing when I stepped into the room. The bright light of my crystal shined more vivid than any of the glyphs and caused a few of the citizens present to shield their eyes.

When I put it away, most of them recovered and went about their business. Some, however, kept a careful eye on me as I walked through the Dark Market. I was amazed at how diverse it was. Citizens from every race in Eto seemed to live here with the city above oblivious to their presence. While most had blue nameplates, some had green like mine. I spotted a few folks walking from one side of the market to the other who had a bounty tag, although none as costly as my own.

Folks whispered to one another as I passed, but no one stopped to talk to me or ask me questions. I tried to stop some people, but they ignored me and hurried away. When I reached the center of the market, I spun in a circle a few times to take everything in, stopping when my stomach growled loudly enough for others to hear.

I found a food stall on the far end of the market. My nose

sniffed it out. If I weren't also incredibly thirsty, my mouth would have watered at the sight of dozens of fire-roasted kebabs waiting to be purchased. I studied the meat skewers closely, wondering what type of meat it was. Glares from the vendor, a dirty looking satyr, stopped me.

"How much for two?" I asked.

"Ten pieces," the satyr answers, his gruff voice sounding more like a growl.

"Ten pieces? For some street meat? You must be kidding." I fingered through my coin pouch, noticing a few unsavory characters eyeing it greedily. Pulling out a few coins, I untied it and slid it into my inventory.

"Fifteen pieces."

"I'll give you seven," I responded.

"Twenty pieces. Unless you don't want to eat."

I sighed at the angry man and looked around some for another food stall but couldn't find anything I would want to eat. His seemed to be the only one serving already cooked food. I handed over twenty pieces and slipped the rest of the loose coins in my pocket, claimed my meal, and sulked away while the vendor counted the coins.

"Come back again soon," he mumbled, but I was too hungry and weary to offer a witty reply.

I found an empty corner of the room where I ate my meal in peace, cringing some from the peppered meat, too spicy for my tastes. I looked around at the crowd of citizens, hoping to find a friendly face. Friendship, however, seemed like a luxury few down here could afford.

3

Sated, albeit still a bit hungry and thirsty, I continued to explore the bustling market looking for information. I tried to approach every green nameplate I spotted, but none of them would acknowledge me. The vendors weren't interested in trading information, even for coin. They only wanted to gouge me by offering prices for goods three times what I would pay on the streets above.

On the far end of the market, near a collection of splintered and cracked tables, a makeshift bar served as a watering hole for residents. As I approached, those sitting there stopped whispering to one another and turned their attention to me, some greed in their eyes suggesting I was easy prey to be robbed blind.

Clutching my inventory bag to make it harder for anyone to pickpocket me, I made my way to a counter and ordered a mug of water for five pieces. Remembering the meat vendor, I didn't argue about the price and paid for it in full, despite water being offered for free in all the pubs and bars above ground.

Sitting in a far corner, I spotted a group of folks my age, most with green nameplates, some with bounties. I was curious about them congregating together. Others with similar nameplates to mine seemed more isolated, but this group was intent on discussing something important, and they all wore identical clothing — dark brown trousers and black hooded shirts.

In the center of the group, a silver-haired young man, a human, leaned over a rolled out bit of parchment. His nameplate, <<*Merrill Flax - Lvl 24*>> was tagged with a 413g bounty. The others around him listened as he traced a finger over the document. One by one they dispersed, until he sat alone at the table. He peered around cautiously as he rolled up the paper, caught me looking at him, and briefly chuckled before he left.

I felt compelled to follow him, so I downed the rest of my water and left the bar, moving across the market toward where I had entered, the man only thirty paces away. I struggled to keep an eye on him as others, much taller than me, blocked my view, but spotted him slipping behind a weapons vendor stall and into a narrow crevice I didn't notice before.

Knowing my hammer would catch on the wall, I took it from my belt before following him. I had to exhale forcefully to squeeze through the narrow passage until it opened into a wide hallway extending as far as I could see, illuminated by glyphs every twenty feet or so. The distance between the glyphs left plenty of shadows and places to hide.

There was no sign of the man. In the time it took me to slip into the tunnel, he vanished. I decided to press on, hoping any random direction would be better than returning to the market.

Unsure of where to go, I scanned the ground for any sign of footprints and crept along the tunnel. The eye icon appeared above my head, wide open. Someone was watching me.

The path had multiple rooms branching from it, none with doors. Some led to hallways sloping either up or down. Some had small rooms littered with discarded rubbish. Others had neatly arranged bedrolls. Some looked like rudimentary workshops.

I passed one where a woman fed her infant child, both of them sick, their faces pocked with sores and boils I had never seen before. Queasy, I moved on, not wanting to catch whatever infected them.

In another room, two men slid shoddy iron daggers over whetstones, both ignoring me as I crept by. With no sign of the man I followed, I began to worry. Even with no one in my field of vision, someone was watching me.

I passed one intersection in the tunnel, both directions to my left and right shrouded in darkness, a perfect intersection to hide. With my hammer in hand, I moved into the tunnel to the left searching for Merrill, but when I did, I felt a weight behind me. Someone grabbed my hammer away with one hand. With the other, they raised a knife to my throat, slicing my skin slightly. I felt the sting of the blade and panicked, knowing if I died here, I would be immediately arrested after resurrecting at the graveyard.

"Why are you following me?" a voice whispered in my ear.

I tried to turn around, but he held me firmly in place.

"Answer me, or I'll slit your throat!" he added.

"I'm hiding from the guards. I mean you no harm. I thought you could help," I said, trying to speak as gently as possible to avoid his blade slicing my neck deeper.

"What made you think I could help you?"

"Our nameplates. They're the same. And the others you met with at the bar seemed to be following you."

He removed the blade from my throat. I rubbed my neck where it once was and felt wet and warm blood on the palm of my hand. Before I could turn around and talk to him again, I heard a pop followed by a hiss. Black smoke filled the entire corridor, blinding me.

"I can't help you," Merrill whispered. When the smoke

cleared, he was gone. I crouched again to activate the stealth eye above me. The eye was firmly closed. No one was watching me anymore. How did he escape so quickly? I didn't hear him flee. No footprints in the loose sand revealed his direction. All that remained was my hammer at my feet.

I didn't want to move further into the tunnel. Already, it began to wind in various directions, fork, and split. Not wanting to get lost, I claimed my hammer and returned to the market where vendors were already starting to close for the day. I had no idea what time it was or how long I had been underground. Without the chime of the cathedral bells signaling the opening and closing of business and the evening curfew, I had no idea where I should go or what I should do.

I bought more meat from the vendor, not arguing with the now ten pieces price he set for me, and got some water and a mug of clear liquor from the bar, the water tasting dirty and the alcohol stinging my throat.

Watching as the market emptied out, I spotted a few citizens lingering in one corner or another, setting up camp for the night. Without the body heat of hundreds of citizens, the room became cold. Magelight glyphs flickered until their light extinguished. I shuffled to the nearest wall of the room, hiding behind an abandoned vendor stall, where goods were packed up and taken with the merchant, and munched on the gamey meat skewers, chasing the peppered meat taste away with water.

Using my inventory bag as a pillow, I tried to fall asleep. Any attempt to rest, though, proved futile. Every sound in the dark room woke me. I worried about thieves who would try to steal my coins or my crystal. I cursed myself for revealing the money and the gem so quickly, as though I held a sign over my head reading "please rob me," for the entire underground to see.

I did this for three days and nights. During the day, I explored outward, finding seven more tunnels leading away from the marketplace, most ending at dead ends, others blocked by rubbish, furniture, or armed citizens who refused to let me pass.

At night, I clutched my inventory bag and slept on a bedroll I purchased from one of the vendors for 50 pieces, leaving me with an ever-dwindling coin pouch, now only holding seven guilders and some change.

I also had a few lesser gems and tried to pawn them to the enchanting stand, but he refused to buy them. His wares were already more advanced than anything the gems could produce, featuring Journeyman and Expert glyphs I wouldn't know how to create. They required advanced etching techniques I wasn't allowed to learn. The craftsman, an elderly gnome, scoffed at me when I asked if he would make me his apprentice, holding his bulbous nose up at me as though the request was beneath him.

I spent another two nights in the Dark Market before I spotted Merrill again, this time sporting a black eye and drinking alone at a table. I sat on a bench opposite him, afraid to talk to him. This seemed a place where killing someone in front of witnesses would be tolerated.

He glared at me while nurturing a mug of warm liquor, and snarled, "You're still alive? That's surprising."

I didn't know how to respond. The man frightened me. As I observed his face, I saw a spiderweb of scars, one sliced across his chin, another gashed across his eyebrow and down his cheek, and a third over the bridge of his nose.

"At a loss for words? I would be too, in your shoes."

He waved me over to join him and signaled the bartender to bring me a mug of booze. I accepted it, graciously. The stuff tasted like acidic piss, but it warmed me up in a cavern too chilly for my liking.

I imagined what he thought of me. Five days underground hadn't been kind. I'd lost weight from lack of food. My hair, pulled back and secured by braids at my temples, began to frizz out for want of a wash. Already, my shaved face formed a thick stubble. I must have started looking more like a dwarf than I did when I arrived. And I stank to high heaven, having spent the last few nights sleeping in filth, relieving myself in a random chamber off the market where everyone, by unspoken agreement, chose to go, and not washing any muck off me I managed to collect.

"You're not going to leave me alone, are you?"

I shook my head.

"Why's that? What makes you think I can help you?"

"Because, aside from the vendors, you're the only one who has said a word to me since I arrived."

He swilled his drink and tapped it on the table, signaling the bartender for more, and impatiently drummed his fingers on the splintered wood while analyzing me.

"What did you do to earn that bounty?" he asked me.

"I killed a traveler who robbed and attacked a friend."

"Must have been some friend for you to throw your freedom away. She pretty?"

I nodded.

Merrill smirked, taking a sip from his now filled mug. "And what is it you want from me?"

"I need to know how to clear my bounty, whatever it takes. And I think you know how I can do it," I said.

"What makes you think that?"

"Because last time I saw you, your bounty was 413 guilders. Now it's 397. You're paying it off. I'd like to know how."

Merrill gulped his drink and hissed through his teeth as it burned its way down his throat. He reached over and grabbed the mug I wasn't drinking from, swallowed it down, and stood up, shuffling a bit as the alcohol appeared to affect him. "Come with me."

I followed him back into the tunnel from the other day to the dark intersection where he threatened to slice my throat. I still had a scab from his blade and spent the last five days worried it might get infected, despite washing it with liquor.

Where I turned left before, he now turned right and vanished into the shadows. I hesitated, wondering again how he disappeared so quickly. Then his hand reached out from the darkness and grabbed me by the collar, yanking me after him.

My vision blurred as he dragged me behind him. Not able to see, I nearly lost my footing as we twisted and turned through a maze of invisible tunnels. When I felt I might fall, he pulled me up with great force and sent me tumbling forward. As I landed on my hands and knees, the shroud around us dissipated. I found myself on a smooth, tiled ebony floor in an intricately constructed tunnel, cleaner and more beautiful than anything I had seen in Steamtown before, save the inside of the Grand Cathedral.

Ahead of me, a massive door blocked our way. Carved into the wood, the divine symbol of Noctra, the night goddess, glowed. I stood up and brushed myself off. Looking at the symbol of the moon with a dagger across it, I waited for Merrill's instruction.

"Wait here," he mumbled. "And don't wander. You'll get lost."

He whispered something into the door, words I couldn't make out, and it cracked open for him, but quickly sealed and locked after he entered. I thought about his warning not to wander. I couldn't retrace my way back to the market even if I wanted to, so I stood patiently, then sat down against the wall and counted the coins that remained in my pouch. I dared not remove the divine crystal, though, knowing how valuable it was. The other gems, a collection of quartz, opals, and ambers, would barely sell for a guilder if I could sell them at all. They were as common as polished river rock or sea glass.

I looked at the door some more, banging the back of my head into the tiled wall out of boredom. The thick wooden door operated mechanically. Massive gears at the top rotated when Merrill entered, sliding the doors open, rather than to push them outwards. I admired the ingenuity in the design and imagined the number of engineers required to construct it.

What felt like hours passed by the time the doors opened again. Merrill slipped through. This time, he wasn't alone. Two men and a woman followed, the three of them armed.

I shot to my feet and raised my hammer, afraid I would have to defend myself. They responded in turn, pointing their blades at me, daring me to attack.

"None of that," Merrill barked at them. "Put your weapons down. He's just scared."

Merrill approached me, placed his hand on my hammer, and pushed it back down to my side. "You're not in danger here," he said.

"Where are we?" I asked. "What is this place?"

"This, young dwarf, is the front entrance to Steamtown's illustrious and infamous thieves guild."

"You mean you all live here? What are your mandates?"

They all laughed at me, but I didn't know why. All citizens had mandates, whether they followed them or not. Despite the green shine of our nameplates, we were citizens, not travelers.

"Dwarf, we have no mandates," one of them muttered, a level 18 male gnome named Horji Thith.

"Ignore him, Delmen. All you need to know is that you asked for help and, after talking with the Crow, we're offering it. All you have to do is say yes, pay the initiation, and join us. We'll have that bounty cleared in no time."

Horji snickered, but Merrill interrupted him. "Well, maybe not in no time, but with some hard work, you'll soon pay it off. Plus we'll train you to go above ground again. It's either us, trying your chances with the assassin's guild, or back to the market until you run out of money and die. What'll it be?"

I cringed at the idea of the assassin's guild. I got in this mess by killing someone. Murdering more people wouldn't help, nor was I the type. I looked Merrill in the eyes, one black and swollen, then considered his associates, who all looked repulsed by the idea of me joining them. "Why me?"

"Why anyone?" Merrill asked. "You show promise. Not only did you escape capture after killing a traveler, something none of us weep over, but you found the Dark Market, and managed to stay alive for five days while keeping all of your gold, and that gem in your bag. Most people who end up down here aren't so resourceful. We could use a man like you, despite your current limitations."

"My current limitations?" I asked.

"Yes. You can't stealth worth a damn, you can't fight, and you certainly can't pick locks, but don't worry. We'll train you." Merrill turned around and leaned into the door, whispering the same words he uttered before, inaudible to me. The heavy wooden doors slid open, with the sound of wood scraping against stone sending chills down my spine.

"So what's the initiation fee?"

"That gem you're carrying is more than enough to cover it. With the surplus, we'll even give you some gear to get you started. Do you accept? You have until the doors close to decide."

The divine crystal burning a hole in my bag felt even more cumbersome. I didn't know what other use I could make of it, so I pulled it out and spun it around briefly in my fingers. The crystal shined in contrast with the ebony tiles. The light reflected off the six daggers still ready to strike me down.

I handed the gem over to Merrill, sighing in the process, wondering if I would ever see another in my life. The dream of etching a rune into it to create an enchant faded, as quickly as the light faded when Merrill slipped it into his bag.

"Very good, come with me." He quickly slipped through the closing doors while the other three headed in the opposite direction, sheathing their daggers before they disappeared into the wall of fog hiding the guild's location.

I slipped through the doors, too, just before they slammed shut, and found myself in an oversized chamber, twice the size and with a roof twice as high as the Dark Market. Unlike the dry and stale air of the market, though, here it was damp and dank, with chilled moisture in the air that bit at my exposed forearms. I shivered, rolling my sleeves down to protect them from the cold.

"Don't worry about the cold. You'll get used to it," Merrill said as he guided me across a stone bridge that extended above an underground river, flowing rapidly and churning around large boulders dotting the riverbed.

He stopped in the middle and turned to me. "Welcome to the thieves guild, Delmen. Before we go any further, I'll lay out some of the ground rules you'll need to know."

"You mean mandates?"

He chuckled again at the mere mention of the word. "No, not mandates. You won't be reassigned to manual labor or imprisoned for violating them. Our rules are more absolute. If you break them, you will be immediately expelled from the guild. Any benefits or rewards you earn before then, though, are yours to keep.

"First," he said, "we are a bunch of thieves, but we're not heartless. Under no circumstances do we steal from one another, or the poor. That includes those living in the underground and those living above. We are not travelers going from door to door, down one close and up the next, stealing from folks merely trying to make rent. Do you understand?"

I nodded. It was a sensible rule that I appreciated. I couldn't imagine stealing from someone like Meridia. I've also been victimized by travelers taking from me, who nearly cost me my home and shop.

"Second, we do not steal from the assassin's guild. In return, they do not honor contracts set on us. This is a mutually beneficial arrangement. That brings me to rule number three. We are not an assassin's guild. We do not kill unless in self-defense. You can't break into someone's home, slit their throat, and rob them blind. If you can't steal something without being caught, don't steal it. Understood?"

I nodded, both listening to him and checking out my surroundings. Once I got used to the roar of the river below, I felt comfortable and safe again for the first time all week. Knowing that no one here would steal from me, kill me, or turn me in to the guards made me imagine a life as a thief, however distasteful I found it.

Merrill continued walking. I followed until we crossed the bridge and passed through a large archway into another chamber, the same size as the former but without the river echoing off the walls. A few people occupied the room, reading books, studying maps, tending weapons and gear, or sleeping in cots carved into the walls, like tombs hewn into the stone.

"Lastly, and this is the fun part, you will be rewarded for all items you pilfer during your various jobs. I would strongly recommend you not sell stolen goods yourself. Folks in the market know you came with me and will see you as a guild member, and few of them deal in stolen wares. You can fence them to Rasha outside the guild vaults. She pays roughly a quarter of market value."

"That seems a little low," I said.

"It's low for a reason. Stolen goods are marked. Only Rasha and a few other fences throughout the city know how to unload marked goods. And the guild needs to make money somehow."

We walked across the room and took a seat at a rickety table near a hearth that burned bright and hot. The heat from the fire chased away the lingering cold in the room.

"You haven't told me how I could clear my bounty," I said.

"No, I haven't, and it doesn't matter now. But since you

mentioned it, bounty removal is a service reserved only for higher ranked members of the guild. You're now an initiate. After you earn your keep, do some jobs for us, and prove your loyalty to the guild, you'll be promoted. The ranks are Initiate, Prowler, Burglar, Operative, Captain, Ringleader, Master Thief, and the High Crow, our leader. I'm a Master Thief in the guild. At the Operative rank, you can engage Rasha and other fences scattered throughout the city to start paying off your bounty."

I started to ask a question, but Merrill stopped me. "Before you ask, clearing your bounty is costly. Assuming you don't create more bounty, which you might if anyone catches you robbing them, it'll cost you 5,000 guilders to pay it down."

My heart skipped a beat when he mentioned the amount. I was accustomed to a weekly rental for my shop and flat of a few guilders a week, but 5,000 seemed nearly impossible to obtain. It was extortion.

Merrill chuckled. "Don't worry too much about the amount. When you're an operative of the guild, you'll have your chance at high-profit scores."

He stood up, stretched his back, and yawned a little. "Enough questions for now. It's nearly mid-day. You should get some rest. Your training starts in the morning. Just grab any empty bed you find. Everything's clean down here. You can bathe and relieve yourself in the next room, but don't wander too far. Our guild hall is vast, and you can easily get lost."

I had so many more questions. And I still hated the idea that I had to become a robber to earn my freedom. I missed my home. I missed Meridia and wondered how she was faring. The traveler I killed would have resurrected by now. I hoped he didn't go back to finish what he started.

Following Merrill's advice, I wandered into the next room, a tidy but wide-open area with pipes running along the walls. Chains dangled down. I pulled one, and hot water sprayed out, running over the floor and into a basin in the middle of the room where it drained.

There were no curtains for privacy, but I didn't care. I had heard of hot showers before but never expected to find one at my disposal. Another guild member, a human, strode in from the other room and unabashedly stripped out of his clothes. He ignored me completely as he set to bathing himself, sighing a little as the hot water cleaned him.

I decided to do the same and stripped out of my muck-saturated clothing. I didn't realize how dirty I was until I observed my clean skin under my clothes. Picking up a bar of soap from a nook in the wall, I scrubbed with such force it began to sting and alternated between bathing myself and cleaning my clothes until I was satisfied enough dirt was rinsed away.

Others, less grimy than me, came in and out in a few minutes, but I lingered for at least twenty until I was as clean and relaxed as I had been in a long time. I pulled the chain above my head to stop the water, leaving me cold and dripping without a towel to dry myself.

"Here," a woman called out. "Initiates always forget the first time."

I spun around and caught a towel with my face before I could see who spoke to me. She sounded a fair bit like Meridia, with a soft voice and a gentle tone that surprised me. I expected all members of the guild to be rough and stern, like Merrill and Horji.

When I dried my face and arms, I wrapped the towel around my waist to protect my modesty. The woman in front of me, a towel wrapped around her torso, wasn't of any race I had seen before, but I had heard of them. She was Lycary, a wolf-woman, native to Ralta, a nation on the other side of Eto.

Light grey fur covered her entire body. Her ears, pointed like a hunting dog, stood out from a thick head of smooth, silver hair. I had heard stories in one pub or another of Lycary, and how they looked more animal than human, but aside from some ridges above her eyes and upturned eyebrows, she appeared mostly human.

"Thank you," I said, stuttering a little, embarrassed and mostly naked.

"Anytime, Initiate," she said before returning to the front room. I caught her nameplate before she left. <<Vasilia -- Lvl 14>>. She didn't have a surname, unlike most citizens in Steamtown. I followed her back into the common room. Most people had crawled into one sleeping cubby or another after washing themselves. The table near the hearth had some food placed there, most already eaten. I found a few morsels remaining, and some steamed greens that I quickly ate. A bowl on the table had some coins in it to pay for the food.

I turned around and spotted Vasilia watching me from her cubby. I took a few coins out of my bag, five pieces in all, and added them to the bowl. She smiled, nodded, and turned over to go to sleep.

I, too, thought I should sleep. As Merrill said, it was the middle of the day in the city above us. Not used to being awake all night, I felt exhausted. I stretched my wet clothes over a rack near the fire along with dripping garments belonging to other guild members, found an empty cubby, and crawled in.

I was pleased with the room in it, and how the heat from the nearby fire left the stone feeling warm to the touch. The many sleeping holes in this room seemed to be sized for humans, the dominant race in Steamtown, so a dwarf like me occupied only half the length of it. The combination of heat, a warm shower, the food, and five nights of restless sleep in the market caught up to me. I fell asleep without realizing it, without knowing how tired I was, tucked in and covered by a thick wool blanket softer than my scratchy linen sheets at home.

4

I woke up to the sound of people clamoring throughout the room. Everyone had started to prepare for a night packed with all sorts of thievery despite seven or eight of us still sleeping.

Vasilia, near the hearth, saw me stirring and waved me over. I got out of the bed, not remembering my state of undress, and the now-dry towel around my waist dropped to the floor. I rushed to pick it up and wrap it around my waist again, but she didn't seem to notice or care one bit.

My clothes were dry now, anyhow, and I slipped them on.

"You seem an odd type for the thieves guild, Delmen. Mind if I ask how you found your way here?" she asked.

"The same way as you, I suppose." I pointed at her green nameplate with a bounty attached, twice the size of mine.

"Did the traveler you killed deserve it?" She slid the blade of one of her daggers over a flat grinding stone on the table.

"Absolutely. He attacked someone I cared for very dearly."

"Good. I never met a traveler being killed who didn't invite it. I don't know why the queen lets them get away with half of the crap they do. It's like they're in charge here."

I agreed with her. Most citizens in Steamtown felt the

same way she did, but few dared to speak their mind, especially since travelers helped us earn a living. Without them, the influx of cheap goods to buy wouldn't exist, and the market district would dry up and wither away. Our city catered to them, despite their abuses.

"Glad to see we're on the same page," she said, standing up and sliding her chair away. She sheathed her daggers and turned to leave the room. "By the way, Merrill was looking for you. Just follow the hallway past the showers until it ends, then take a right. His quarters are the first door."

She started to leave but turned around. "And Delmen? Good luck with your training."

Her voice sounded sarcastic, almost sinister when she wished me luck and I worried what training Merrill had in store for me. I also knew I shouldn't keep him waiting, so I finished dressing and took a few bites of food on the table, dropping in some coins from my dwindling supply to pay for it, and made my way deeper into the guild hall. Merrill was correct in telling me not to wander. While the path never forked, I passed dozens of intersections leading off in every direction, before I reached the end of the central tunnel, which stopped abruptly not at a wall but a steep drop-off into a crevasse. I kicked a loose stone into the gap and counted to ten before I heard a plop, as the rock hit water.

Turning right, I walked down the hallway, sticking as close to the wall as possible until I reached the first door. The glow of a fire slipped out from under the door and cast a mirage of dancing shadows on the ground.

Knocking, I heard Merrill yell for me to enter. With no doorknob to turn, I pressed my hand against an emblem of a silver crow carved into the door. It slid forward, and a machine clicked, latching onto the frame and pushing it into the wall.

Inside the room, Merrill sat in an over-stuffed chair, spinning the divine crystal I gave him in his fingers, observing it with due respect and admiration, as though it were the most priceless thing in the world.

"You know," he said, "when you showed up last week clutching this, I couldn't believe it. Half the pisspots in the market likely thought you stole it, but one look at you and I could tell you were no thief. Then I got to thinking. You escaped the guard, you survived down here where most would have their throats slit on the first night, and you found your way to me. You're either very, very lucky or you're blessed by Noctra."

I entered the room without saying a word and glanced around. Although sparsely decorated, it spoke of a man of means and wealth. The furniture alone looked more like it belonged in a palace, not in a dank cavern.

"I figure it's some combination of both. How about you, Delmen? What do you think?"

"Most definitely both," I mumbled. The man still intimidated me. I hesitated to say something that might anger him. He put the gem in a jewelry chest on an end table next to him and shot up.

"Let's say we go find out the answer. It's time for you to start your training!"

He sped out of the room, or more rightly took advantage of his full stride, forcing me to jog a bit to keep up with him. Making a right out of his door, I followed him for what felt like forever as we wound our way through the nonsensical underground maze.

If not for my keen underground eyesight, a trait all dwarves share in common, there were times when I would have lost him, but after a few minutes of rushing through the guild hall, we reached a stone door.

Merrill rattled on the door with his fingers. It slid open, revealing a room so absent light even my eyes couldn't pierce through the darkness. It felt about as dark as the market or the glen under North Bridge at night.

He grabbed me by the collar and tossed me through the door, sending me tumbling to my hands and knees.

"Go ahead. Sneak your way out," he said as he tossed a bundle at my feet. Merrill stepped back, pulled a chain on the wall, and the door slammed shut.

What the hell is he playing at? I asked myself as I collected the leather bundle. I couldn't see the contents of it but felt small metal objects with curved ends of varying sizes — lock-picking tools.

The moment I stood up, a red light shone and nearly blinded me, followed by the sound of gongs that left a ringing in my ears so loud I thought I might never hear again. I remembered what Merrill instructed, about sneaking my way through, and crouched to be more stealthy.

Above me, the eyeball icon appeared, first opened, then slowly began to close. The golden ring around me projected outward a few feet from my body, although it offered no illumination for me to see by.

I inched forward a few steps, but the sound of my boots against the ground sent echoes down the chamber, each clacking noise opening the eye a little more until, after only ten feet, the eye opened all the way, the bright red light blinded me, and the gong sounded. I covered my ears and closed my eyes, but when I opened them, I felt the door behind me.

I hadn't made any progress, and any sort of detection magically transported me back to the beginning of the training area. After teleporting three times back to the beginning, making more progress than I had the first time, I took off my boots, putting them in my inventory for safe keeping.

I crept along again, the cold floor turning my toes numb. While the eye icon remained closed, every time I moved forward it opened slightly, but I found if I crept slowly enough and stayed as quiet as possible, it never widened completely. Ten paces. Twenty paces. Forty paces. The eye slightly opened and closed, like a tired man's eyes trying to stay awake.

As I pressed forward, guided only by my hand against the wall, I was surprised to find the tunnel illuminate some behind me after ten to fifteen steps I took. Barely enough to see by, the magical lights caused a long shadow to descend the hall until everything ended in darkness. I sneaked forward on the balls of my feet until I felt with my hands a thick, wooden door with an iron handle, the first such door I'd found in the thieves guild not operated by machines.

I rattled the handle and pulled at the door, but it was stuck, locked in place. It was a mistake to make so much noise with it. The eyeball shot open and blazed above me like a raging fire. Red light. Gongs. I was back at the beginning.

I cursed in frustration, took out my hammer, and banged it into the door, triggering the whole experience over again. The gong vibrating in my ears felt as though it was scrambling my brain. Merrill left me here. He certainly wasn't going to release me only twenty minutes in. I needed to get a grip.

Breathing deeply to calm myself, I crouched and padded my way to the door again. This time, instead of rattling the door handle, I unrolled the lockpicking tools, felt around for the keyhole, and inserted two tools, not sure what might happen next.

A big square opened up in my field of vision, and time seemed to slow to a halt. Within the square, I could move a sturdy lockpick while another probe gripped and turned the lock. A label at the top of the square informed me it was a novice lock.

As I struggled to turn both metal tools, the eyeball above my head started to open slightly. If I weren't careful, I'd have to start all over, so I took my time and focused, beads of sweat forming on my brow and dampening my palms. The wetness made gripping the tools difficult and delayed me all the more.

At last, after twisting and turning both implements, the

lock rotated and clicked. The door, previously secured in place, glided open to reveal the next room. A silent bell jingled, and the hallway behind me went dark as the mage-light glyphs embedded into the wall went out one by one.

<<Sneak rank 3>>
<<Lockpicking rank 2>>

The next hallway, not cast in shadow, was tiled like the rest of the guild hall, with black stone extending until the corridor forked and curved beyond what I could see. As I stepped into the hallway, the door behind me slammed shut and startled me. I jumped forward, breaking stealth, and bit my lip, expecting a loud gong and the reset of the hallway, but none came. I hesitated to press on too quickly. The last tunnel tested my stealth and lockpicking and most definitely tried my patience.

This hallway felt different. I crouched. No eye icon appeared above me, and no golden detection ring wrapped around me. There was no mechanism to catch me sneaking down the path. I took one step forward, cautiously. My heart skipped a beat as the tile below me cracked, as though it were a thin sheet of ice.

I pulled my foot back and tried another tile. The same. Wherever my bare foot landed, the floor began to crumble. I searched as many tiles as I could, but they were all the same, each beginning to crumble and give way, spiderweb-like cracks left in my foot's absence.

I pressed forward, careful not to linger on any tile for too long. After ten steps, I felt I was moving too slowly, and tiles began to splinter and collapse to reveal a bottomless void. I panicked as the ground under me gave way. I grasped for a handhold on the walls, but they were too far apart for me to secure myself. The tips of my fingers scratched into the smooth walls as the entire floor disappeared in the blink of an eye, and I fell. With nothing to grip, I slid down a ravine, holding my breath and squeezing my eyes shut waiting until I struck bottom.

But the bottom never came. I felt solid ground beneath me again and opened my eyes to find myself at the start of the tunnel, with the prior door pressed against my back.

"This is sadistic!" I yelled, wondering if Merrill was somehow watching me, laughing his ass off.

How do they expect me to get by this? *I'm a sturdy dwarf, not a dainty elf.* I wasn't the most nimble creature, more accustomed to firm Steamtown streets and wooden walkways. I didn't know how to climb, or swim, or even dance.

I shrugged. There was no going back. The door behind me was closed with no visible lock to pick. So I pressed forward, this time doing my best to jump quickly from one tile to the next, only as I leaped, the tiles took the full force of my weight and shattered. Absent footing, my leg sank into the hollow ground, sending me tumbling forward. I winced as the ground under my hands and knees broke, sending me plummeting again until the experience reset and I was back at the beginning.

"There has to be some trick to this," I mumbled. The hallway, about as wide as I was tall, seemed to challenge me. There was no telling how far it went, but if I managed to make it to the fork in the path, I could hold onto the split in the wall and buy myself some time to decide what direction to take.

Lying down on my belly, I began to worm my way down the path, careful not to put too much weight on a single tile. This proved a better option for me. Without the full load of my heavy legs or large hands, the tiles didn't break as quickly. I made steady progress, able to shuffle forward on my forearms, my weight spread across three or more tiles.

I reached the fork in the path and paused for a moment,

careful not to even breathe, lest my expanding belly caused the tiles to give way.

Down the left-hand side of the path the ground remained the same brittle tiles. Down the right, I spotted gaps in the path, dotted by lilypad-sized pillars of rock. The right-hand way would require I jump from one post to the next, something I felt I wouldn't be capable of doing. My legs were too short and slow for the nimble leaps required to press forward.

Instead, I crawled on my belly down the left path until, in another forty feet, the way split again, with the same pillared hallway waiting for me. My head sank. I looked back, wondering if I should have taken the other direction, but realized I hadn't gone very far at all. Behind me, the door to the previous challenge was within sight. This was the same intersection.

I knew, then, that I needed to go right, and climbed to my feet, careful to continue moving forward until tile became solid rock, the ground before me empty save the stone pillars I needed to pass.

"Damn it, Delmen, you can do this!" I muttered.

Not knowing how smooth the stone could be, I put my boots back on for the added traction, took one deep breath, cleared my mind, and jumped.

The first stone pillar swayed as my foot landed. I felt the shuddering of rock beginning to crack and crumble under me. If I lingered, it would give way entirely to the void, so I took a second to balance myself before leaping again. And again, and again. It proved more straightforward than I thought. Despite my having never moved like this before, I found a rhythm that made forward progress easier. Leap. Regain balance. Position. Leap. Regain balance. Position. Leap.

Don't forget to breathe.

I smiled when I saw the end of the path, another door blocking my way, and exhaled in relief when I made the final jump, pressing my entire torso into the smooth door, eager to move onto the next trial.

<<Athletics Rank 2>>

I picked the lock, another novice-level barrier, and pushed the door open.

<<Lockpicking Rank 3>>

Ahead of me, another sneaking hallway waited. I stepped forward and crouched. The door behind me closed, blocking my way back. Not that I could go back. I had to keep pressing forward. This was a training area, carefully created by the guild to get me comfortable using the skills I would need to thieve my way to freedom.

The eyeball appeared above me and my golden detection circle extended outward. As I moved forward in darkness, I felt the narrow hallway begin to widen until the room became more extensive than the Dark Market. I stuck to the center of the room, creeping forward while the eye above me flickered, opening slightly with every careful step.

I spotted faint orbs of light floating around the chamber with thin, blue detection circles extending around them. They moved from left to right, sweeping the room, scanning for any sign of an intruder. I recognized them instantly as detection glyphs, something I wasn't allowed to create at my enchanting level, but objects I knew were designed to detect trespassers.

As an enchanter, I knew the glyphs were dumb. They were a poor substitute for sturdy locks, guards, and watchmen. Unlike guards, they couldn't think. If someone was hiding behind an object, like a wall, door, or piece of furniture, they could go undetected. As one approached me, I backed up against the door so that our detection circles didn't overlap.

I studied all the floating spheres until I spotted both a pattern and some areas to hide behind — stalagmites on the ground broad enough to hide my entire body. The detection rings around the glyphs didn't extend beyond the massive spikes.

I waited another minute until the glyph closest to me passed, and then sneaked forward as quickly as I could to the first stalagmite just in time to avoid the next glyph, one of a dozen or so, pass by. Just as it did, the first glyph circled back again. As it approached, I pressed my back into the stone pillar and slid around the spike to remain hidden. As the second glyph started to return, I spotted another pillar and bounced forward, watching the eye above me for any sign of detection. It was nearly completely open by the time I reached the next stalagmite. I crouched as low as I could and moved around it until I was hidden in shadow.

<<Sneak rank 4>>

Looking ahead for a sign that this challenge would end soon, I felt puzzled. In the distance, I spotted two stationary orbs fixed in place near the doorway. Their detection rings overlapped to block my way.

Gravel littered the ground. I would make too much noise if I tried to approach them. In a safe spot, out of reach of the floating orbs, I took a moment to decide what to do. The room had no other visible exit. I recalled my enchanter's training. Sure, I wasn't allowed to create the glyphs I now faced, but I knew about them. Detection glyphs were among the first glyphs expert enchanters were allowed to craft.

I recalled the multiple forms and the traits of stationary and mobile glyphs until I remembered the third type, the hybrid, that could be set at a specific location and enchanted to scan the area around it whenever a movement was detected. They returned to their anchor point only when not discovering anything.

I had to distract the glyphs, which meant creating noise well away from where I actually was. Feeling around the ground, I found a stone large enough to create a decent echo when tossed.

I waited for my chance, when all of the floating glyphs were far enough away from me, and moved ahead, abandoning the safety of the stalagmite closest to the door. Right when my detection ring was about to intersect the anchored glyphs when the eyeball above me was nearly opened, I tossed the rock as far as I could to the far side of the room. When it struck the wall, the echo it made startled me, and while the moving glyphs continued to scan in their predetermined pattern, the anchored ones rotated and scurried off toward the source of the noise.

I had my chance, my brief window before the glyphs reset, and moved as quickly as I could toward the door. It was bolted shut, secured by another novice lock that proved more natural to pick now that I had gotten used to it.

Within seconds, the door was opened. I slipped through, just before the anchored glyphs returned.

<<Sneak rank 5>>

I was no longer underground. Instead, I was in a wooded area. The moon shone bright overhead, dispersed by a haze that lingered in the air from Steamtown's many forges and factories. Even though a thick layer of shrubbery blocked my view of the whole area, I knew where I was — the Royal Gardens happened to be one of my favorite spots in the city. I was upset the training put me at risk, where the previous challenges merely reset if I was detected, but I felt some relief at being outdoors again and inhaled the scent of fresh flowers that littered the garden's paths.

After being underground for a week, I realized I had forgotten how sweet flowers smell, even when they only partially masked the city's stink. I didn't have too much time to linger and enjoy the gardens, though. I was being trained, and Merrill wouldn't have arranged this if he knew the gardens would be merely a moonlight stroll in the park.

The gardens, the pride of the High Mile, served as a buffer between the rabble of the poorer districts and the aristocracy, the governor's mansion, and the Queen's Palace.

I didn't know how to proceed. Merrill wouldn't require I sneak all the way back to North Bridge and enter the Dark Market. There had to be a different test here.

I turned around to check the closed door behind me, only there was no door. A wall of smooth rock replaced it, as though I had been transported here. On the ground, a scrap of paper was held in place by a stone.

Delmen, your goal is marked by a red crystal with the symbol of Noctra, the dagger piercing the crescent moon. Tap the gem three times with your hammer to reveal a secret entrance. If the guards catch you, your membership with the guild is rescinded. You have until sunrise. -M

I crumpled the paper up and shoved it in my pocket, furious that Merrill would make me do this knowing the size of the bounty I had, knowing that capture meant reassignment to the Stockades.

Having no other choice, I pressed on and scrambled through the thorn bushes whose brambles scratched my arms and tore at my cheeks, until I reached an open path winding through the gardens. I scanned up and down for signs of guards, spotting a couple of torches up the hillside. I squinted, trying to see how many guards there were and whether they were simple patrols or Governor Law's enforcers, but I couldn't tell.

Knowing my boots would make too much noise, I removed them to my inventory and took my first step out onto the open path, careful to remain in stealth. Out in the open with few shadows to hide me, my stealth ring expanded halfway up the hillside. The sound of rustling bushes drew the guards' attention, and they moved down the hill toward me.

I had three choices — hurry down the path away from the guards, retreat into the bushes behind me where any twig snapping under my hands or leaves crushing under my knees would risk detection, or push forward into a grove ahead, hiding amidst the trees. Like the previous three rooms I trained in, did I prefer room number one, number two, or number three?

I looked down the path leading away from the guards and spotted more torches in the distance, so I opted for the only training scenario where I wasn't caught and left the path to hide amidst the garden's many trees. Secure behind a thick-trunked tree, I breathed as quietly as possible while my heart pounded in my ears.

"What was it? What did you see?" one of the approaching guards asked his partner.

"I didn't see anything. It sounded like someone was in the bushes."

"Don't be daft. It was most likely a feral cat or something."

"I know cats, and they don't make that much noise. Were there any notices tonight?"

"Nope. Just the same ones from earlier in the week. Delmen MacDougall is still at large, although he's most likely dead in a ditch somewhere, and that elf neighbor of his, missing from her shop."

"You mean Meridia Alandria? What's that about? It wasn't her fault what happened."

I perked my ears, now anxious to hear the rest of their conversation.

"I don't know. She never opened her shop the next morning. Even her house was locked. If you ask me, the snatchers got her. Or perhaps another victim of the Bean family. She could have run away."

"Maybe the dwarf took her?"

"Who cares? I wouldn't want to be him now, though. If we ever catch him, it's the stocks for sure. Now let's get back to our post. Captain will kill us if we're gone too long."

As the guards walked away, I felt both furious and anxious at the same time, enraged that they didn't care to find Meridia, and panicked over what happened to her. I tried to rescue her from the traveler but managed to ruin her life in the process. I berated myself over my actions, realizing then why the mandates should have been followed. I needed answers, and that meant getting back to the guild hall and talking to Merrill.

Already, the sky started to turn brighter. I didn't have much time to make it to the other side of the gardens before the sun rose and sneaking became impossible, so I spun around and moved as quickly as I could through the grove that covered half the park.

5

The gardens were a desolate place at night, lacking all the hustle and bustle of evening revelers, travelers and citizens alike. On a breezy evening, when weather permitted, hosts of people occupied every free patch of grass on the great lawn in the southern half of the park, eager to enjoy the fresh air and cooler temperatures outside their crammed closes or tiny flats. Travelers also used the park, either to reach the Queen's Palace or to practice their pickpocketing skills. As a result, guards were always stationed there in droves, not necessarily to catch the travelers, but to provide them with a challenge, one I never understood until now.

As I reached the center of the gardens with the arbor grove behind me and the great lawn ahead, I felt for a moment what travelers might feel — an exuberant rush that came with breaking the law and not getting caught.

Where guards patrolled the central path leading from Commercial Way to the High Mile, the great lawn was unmonitored, save some floating detection glyphs that I hadn't seen before. I never walked the gardens after curfew. That was before I became an outlaw when I always found myself tucked into bed before the final evening bell rang.

I lingered behind a tree while I mapped out in my mind both the cycles the guards followed and the path the glyphs took across the lawn. I realized that getting by the guards wouldn't be a challenge. I just needed to wait until they were facing away from me, both groups headed in opposite directions.

Then I had to rush across the lawn and make it to the central fountain, where I could hide from the orbs.

I dug my fingers into the rough bark of my hiding tree as the guards approached, knowing I had to make a break for it soon. After their next pass, the sun would start to rise. Sneaking would become impossible.

As they turned and walked toward the edges of the garden, I abandoned the tree, crouching to remain hidden in the grove, and waited patiently for my window, when my detection circle wouldn't cross theirs. I padded my way across the path, my bare feet struggling to find purchase on the slick cobblestone walkway. The eyeball above me opened halfway as I grunted, sliding until I reached the grass lawn.

I regained my composure, chastising myself for not being more cautious. One slip almost had me caught. Once the eye icon closed again, I counted the orbs and waited. As the guards reached the perimeter and turned back around, the orbs parted just enough to allow me to zig-zag my way to the middle of the lawn where I hid behind the gilded fountain. I wondered why no one tried to steal the gold but remembered the etchings of the Five Eternals. This was less a fountain and more a shrine, home to many outdoor ceremonies.

I crouched against the cobblestone ground, littered with trash and refuse from a celebration earlier in the day, and waited for a window to open to the far side of the lawn where a small grove of trees could hide me.

<<Sneak Rank 6>>

Counting how long each orb patrolled, I found a gap to slip through and took off as quickly as my legs could carry me, a laughably slow pace compared to the speed the detection glyphs moved.

Huffing for air after forty feet or so, I panicked as the traveling orbs closed in on me. Short on time, I continued to run in stealth before the patrolling guards turned around. All it would take would be a cursory glance across the lawn for them to spot me, or an inch long overlap of my detection circle and a glyph.

Nearly to the trees, I spotted two glyphs approaching from both sides, narrowing the window that would allow me to pass. Despite moving as fast as I could, I was too late. In one last-ditch effort to avoid detection, I dove and rolled, but broke stealth in the process. My detection ring vanished. All the glyphs around me immediately began to vibrate, releasing an ear-splitting shriek, like the sound of a hundred boiling teapots whistling at once. I tried to stealth again but couldn't trigger the eye icon. I knew I was detected.

"Stop in the name of the queen!" I heard a guard yell. Images of what I thought the stockades might be like flashed in my mind, providing me incentive to flee. I slipped into the trees just as the guards on the middle path started to pursue me.

I didn't wait for them to gain ground, and moved deeper into a tightly packed tree stand, much denser than the carefully planned and meticulously manicured arboretum on the other side of the gardens.

<<Athletics Rank 3>>
<<Level-up! Open interface to select rewards.>>

I didn't have time to pay attention to the text clogging my vision, so I ignored it until it faded. Not being able to hide, even in the trees, I ran into the dense wood, searching for

Merrill's red crystal. I heard guards behind me trying to push their way through the thick underbrush, hacking away at it with their swords where I plowed through as best I could, thorny vines and stinging nettles scraping my skin. I was only forty feet or so ahead of them when an unusually thick vine caught my foot and sent me tumbling forward down an embankment.

Try as I might, I couldn't stop myself from rolling over and over like a barrel, spinning down the hill. I reached the bottom with a loud thud that left me dizzy. I heaved, trying to get air back into my lungs. When I came around again, I spotted my target: a small red crystal sticking out of the ground with the mark of Noctra etched into it, grooves filled with a black pigmentation to make the etching stand out.

I crawled to the crystal, wincing as sharp stones, barbs, and dried needles stabbed my palms. Reaching the gem, I pulled my hammer out of my inventory and struck it three times. Each blow by my hammer, the grip now slick with my blood, sounded like a bell chiming, signaling to the guards my precise location.

"He's down the hill! Get him!" I heard a guard yell, but they were both unable and unwilling to descend the slope the same way I did. I panicked, knowing I had little time, with no idea how the crystal was supposed to save me. I stared at it wondering what would happen next, holding my breath in anticipation. Where my hammer struck, the crystal began to splinter. Bits of it broke off and crumbled to dust.

As the guards tried to make their way down the steep slope, the crystal dissolved. When the last of the glass-like stone turned to dust, I heard an audible click of a hatch unlocking and felt a rumble of machinery below me. The ground started to give way, opening downward to a dark abyss. I had no choice but to fall with the doors, landing again with another thud that forced all the air from my lungs.

Once I cleared the trap door, it rose again until it latched in place, then turned to solid stone like the original entrance I took into Dark Market. This time, though, I was without a divine crystal to illuminate my way.

"First chance I get, I'm making myself a magelight glyph," I groaned. Turning onto my back, I felt around trying to figure out where I was. All the while, the area around me still rumbled. I felt the sensation of movement, as though I was carried somewhere. I had no choice but to wait. With four solid walls surrounding me and a gap of two feet between my back and the roof above me, I was stuck in a stifling stone coffin.

After what felt like an eternity and just as I started having trouble breathing for lack of air, the entire stone box surrounding me jolted violently. My feet planted firmly on the bottom of the box. I closed my eyes as the lid cracked open, holding up my hand to shield myself from the brightness of the morning sun.

I stepped out of the stone coffin and gasped. I wasn't underground. I wasn't in Steamtown, either. I was on the shore of the southern lake. The cliffs protecting the city jutted upward behind me.

A few dozen feet away, Merrill and Vasilia waited, sharing a meal between them by the water's edge. I stumbled over, my pants, arms, and hands stained by my own blood, and sat down, exhausted by my ordeal.

"Delmen MacDougall, it's official. You're now 100% an outlaw," Vasilia said between bites of her morning dinner. She looked at me and snarled, although I thought she might be attempting a smile. It was hard to tell with her race since smiling revealed their sharp fangs. "Still, you could have been a little more graceful about it. The guards are going to be on high alert now that they spotted you. It's going to make things rather difficult for all of us."

"Hush, Vasilia," Merrill said. "Or do you forget your training? Your first time out, you didn't even escape the tunnels."

"And how could I? You, oh mighty Master Thief, didn't give me any lockpicks!"

Merrill laughed. "Yeah, I almost forgot about that. How long did I leave you in there?"

"Three days!"

I tried to laugh at them but couldn't muster the energy. I was exhausted. More exhausted than I had ever been in my entire life. And despite not having eaten in hours, I wasn't at all hungry. I just wanted to collapse and fall asleep. Merrill, shooting to his feet, had other plans for me. Both he and Vasilia packed up leftovers from their meal, grabbed me under my arms, and hauled me to my feet.

"Delmen, you didn't show the best performance, but you didn't get caught. There's merit in that alone, so welcome, Initiate, to the Steamtown Thieves Guild."

I staggered after them as they walked down the narrow shoreline toward South Bridge. It didn't seem to faze either of them when we waded through the dirty, knee-deep water. I couldn't imagine they would have me swim the length of the lake to the first close along Commercial Way. I didn't know how to swim, and I feared the aquatic predators supposedly hiding below the surface.

Just as the water reached my chest the two of them stopped. Merrill placed his hand on a polished rock, one a little smoother and more worn compared to the surrounding landscape, and rotated it in multiple directions. I realized he was entering a combination. After one final spin and an audible click, the seamless cliff vibrated. I felt a tugging at my ankles as the cliff wall slid upward to allow water inside, but the opening was slow enough to prevent a strong current to suck us in.

Less than a minute later, we three slipped into Steamtown's underground and the door in the cliff closed. Vasilia, mindful that I was weak, helped me up a gentle slope until we were free of the water. Now in a glyph-illuminated hallway with black tiles lining the floor, ceiling, and walls, I breathed a sigh of relief knowing we were back in the guild.

"Just how many entrances to the underground are there?" I asked both of them.

"We don't know. The Dark Market has only one entrance, but it moves between twenty different locations with no known pattern. No one knows what controls it. As for the Thieves Guild, we have about two dozen fixed entrances and exits scattered around the city. We're certain other factions underground, like the Assassin's Guild, have their own hidden entrances," Merrill said.

"And some people, like Vasilia and me, have ways in and out that we don't share. I'm certain you'll be able to find your own once you have more experience."

"What about the Bean family?" I asked, remembering the guard conversation I heard before.

Merrill stopped dead in his tracks. "How did you hear that name?"

"I overheard some guards talking about them. My friend is missing. They think the Beans took her."

"If that's true, it's unfortunate. I pity anyone taken by them."

"Why? Who are they?"

"That, dwarf, is information, and information costs money."

We reached a dead end in the hallway, a solid wall marked by the symbol of Noctra. Merrill raised his dagger and traced it along the entire symbol until he found a groove in the etching, where he was able to insert his blade up to the hilt. The wall shuddered. Stone scraped against stone, and the hall began to vibrate. I felt the trembles in my entire body, finding it hard to focus on the conversation at hand.

He removed the dagger just before the door disappeared into the ground, opening the way to the heart of the thieves guild hall. Turning left, Merrill guided me back to his private chambers.

I felt frustrated he wouldn't help me. Meridia was in danger. She wasn't dead, sure. If she had been killed, she would have resurrected at the graveyard by now, but I needed to find a way to help her.

"How much?" I asked him before he slipped into his quarters. "I'm the reason Meridia's in this mess. I can't stand by and do nothing."

"I guess that depends on what you'll do with the information. If you just want to know what happened to Meridia and who the Beans are, not much. If you want information to mount a rescue, there's no amount of gold in Steamtown that would convince me to help you."

I didn't want that answer, knowing full well I needed to save Meridia even if it meant risking the stockades.

"Surely the crystal I gave you more than covers a bit of information," I said. I could feel Vasilia tense up as I challenged Merrill. I'd almost forgotten she was still there.

"That crystal you gave me barely covers what we've done for you. Everything you do here costs money. The armor and weapons we will give you, the training, the housing, the water, and the bribes we'll have to pay to calm the guards back down after your antics in the city all add up. You, a mere initiate, are in no position to challenge me to help you any more than I already have."

Merrill stepped back into his room and began to close the door. "But I can't stop you from throwing your freedom away. I won't give you the information you need. I can't stop others in the guild from helping you. You'll still have to pay them, though. Nothing in our guild is free."

He looked frustrated with me but came off as compassionate at the same time, like a father handling a disobedient child. He sealed and locked his door, leaving Vasilia and me alone, her looking weary after a long night of thieving. I was covered in scrapes, bruises, sticky sap, and muck from crawling through the royal gardens.

"Will you help me?" I asked.

"For free? No. But I'll sell you information on what I know about the Beans and whether they took your friend."

"How much, then?"

"Perhaps all of the loot from your first successful heist. I won't discuss anything more until then. For now, you should get yourself cleaned, have some food, then talk to me about leveling up."

She was right. I wasn't going to find Meridia tonight, not in my current state. If the Bean family was some underground group using the tunnels under the city for hiding, I certainly wasn't going to find them. I couldn't even find my way in and out of the guild hall on my own.

An hour later, after I finished cleaning every inch of me, washing my clothes, and feeding on the meager offerings in the common room, I considered the question of leveling up. I knew I had leveled up before. I wasn't always level ten, although I couldn't remember how I achieved that level on my own. Travelers knew how to level. I witnessed one traveler, a frequent customer of mine, go from level 1 to level 18 in the time I knew him, then I assumed he left Steamtown as I never saw him again.

But citizens never leveled. Our mandates forbade it.

"So I'll bite," I said to Vasilia. Her ears perked as she abandoned her task at hand, polishing a goblet she must have stolen that night.

"You want to know how to take advantage of your leveling?" she asked.

"Yes. Is that information free, or will it cost me, I don't know, my shirt."

She laughed, although I could hardly tell. It sounded more like a bark. "You can keep your shirt. Increasing your level makes you more efficient a thief, which can only benefit the guild. Just think 'Interface,' and you'll be able to bring up all the information you need. The rest should be self-explanatory."

I did as she suggested and thought the word. Suddenly, an entire array of text I had never seen before filled my field of vision. Everything else went black. I could no longer see the room around me, although I could still sense the heat from the hearth and feel aches and pains throughout my body from a day of crouching, leaping, crawling, and running. My back, between my shoulder blades, twinged from my tumble down the hillside during my escape from the guards.

The screen broke into four segments. I found when I focused on one, a floating arrow hovered over the area and started to select it. I read *Level Up, Stats, Map, and Inventory.*

I focused on *Level Up* until the arrow selected it, and the four segments faded, replaced with a shade, perhaps a ghost, who spoke to me.

> <<*"Congratulations, Traveler, on reaching level ten. At level nine, you earned five points in Sneak, two points in Athletics, two points in Lockpicking, and one point in One-Handed Weapons. You have favored the way of the rogue. Your stamina and health have increased by five percent. You have also earned two skill points that you can spend on two of the following five improvements."*>>

A list of available options appeared, silver text on a black void. The shade faded from my vision.

> <<*1. Reduce the diameter of your sneak detection orb by 10%.*
> *2. Reduce the sensitivity of your sneak detection orb by 10%.*
> *3. Make lockpicking Novice locks 25% easier.*
> *4. Deal 5% more damage with one-handed weapons.*

5. Run 5% faster with no impact on stamina. >>

"I don't know what to pick. My choices all seem very useful."

Vasilia smirked. I didn't know whether it was because she thought me a dunce or because she used to ask similar questions. "You're a thief now. As a thief, your strengths are sneaking and running. Don't waste points on lockpicking. The tools Merrill gave you can't break, so there's no reason for you to worry about how easy picking locks is."

I nodded. Her suggestions made sense. I recalled my earlier debacle in the Royal Gardens when my detection orb was too large, and I was too slow, so I chose options one and five. A bell dinged in my ear. My nameplate flickered, now reading <<*Delmen MacDougall -- LVL 10 -- 1000g bounty*>>.

Afterward, my interface closed. The room returned to normal with Vasilia finishing her evening chores and preparing for bed. Since I returned to the common room, more and more guild members filed in, some lugging in wares from an evening full of thieving. Others held their heads low having not pilfered anything substantial. While most were human, the group represented many of the races I've met over the years, although I was the only dwarf.

They all shared one thing in common. While they talked and joked among themselves, they ignored me. I was only an initiate, after all. They had no reason to trust me. They didn't even have a cause to like me.

I turned to Vasilia and talked at a whisper out of courtesy for those already in bed. "Do you know what I'll be doing tonight?"

"Anything you want to do is my guess. Your training is over. You can come with me if you like. I have a plant job from an estate house in the High Mile. While I sneak upstairs, you're more than welcome to go to town downstairs."

"How will I know what to take?" I asked.

Horji, the angry gnome from the day before, strode into the room. I felt everyone around me grow tense, including Vasilia. While none of them seemed to like me, it looked like they all actively disliked him.

"Take anything shiny, you ugly dolt," he barked.

"Ignore him," Vasilia said. "He's just angry that anything good to steal is beyond his reach."

Horji's face turned bright red. She touched on a sore spot for him. He barked a weak comeback, something about smelling like a wet dog, and stormed out of the room.

"What's his deal?" I asked her.

"No one knows for sure, but he is all about purity in the thieves guild. Where most of us join out of desperation as you did, he joined out of desire. He comes in here a few times a week to vent his frustrations about the state of the guild, how we disgrace it, and how things used to be better before Merrill ran the show."

"What does the Silver Crow think of it?"

"Who knows. Few of us know who the Silver Crow is. He doesn't live in the guild hall. We're not sure if he is one person or even a man. The Crow only gets involved when something goes wrong, or for the most substantial heists. Even then, he relays all instructions through Merrill."

Vasilia's eyes drooped as she spoke. Her last words were interrupted by a mighty, silent yawn. I realized she was staying up for me.

"So are you with me tonight or what?" she asked.

"Definitely. But can we stop off at my old flat first? I'm hoping it's still empty. There are some things I want to get."

"You mean that chest of gems under your floorboards?"

I felt silly. Of course they knew about my hiding place. They must have fleeced my flat the moment I abandoned it.

"Don't worry," she added. "The chest is still there. We don't steal from Commercial Way or guild members, remember? So long as no one's moved in yet, we can get it first thing tonight."

"Thank you," I said. "I still don't understand why you're helping me so much, but it's appreciated."

"Stop thanking me and go to bed. You're no use to me tomorrow if you're too tired to function. Anyhow, thieving is better with a partner. Two people can always carry more than one."

I couldn't argue with that sentiment, so I retired to my cubby near the fireplace. As I lay in bed, I wondered if this would be my life now. With even the most basic information costing me money paired with the need to buy my way into higher ranks in the guild enough to pay down my bounty, I worried I was delaying the inevitable. Scanning the name-plates around the room, I saw plenty with bounties, none quite as significant as my own, save Vasilia's. I worried I would be a slave to this guild forever, trading restrictive shopkeeper mandates for mounting debt to a guild that would see me housed and fed, but never prosper.

Before I could worry more, though, sleep took me.

6

———

"Come on! You can do it!" Vasilia taunted me, trying to coax me closer to the ledge to waltz over a plank stretching from one side of Crafter's Close to the other. I muttered under my breath. If I knew she would have me jumping rooftops, I would have found a way to get to my flat on the ground despite the risks.

"Easy for you to say. You're part wolf. Dwarves aren't known for acrobatics."

"Come on. I haven't got all night. You're the one who wanted to come here, and this is the safest way."

My knees trembled as I took one step out on the rickety board. I feared it wouldn't hold my weight, not because it looked flimsy, but because it bowed under me. I exhaled, feeling as though expelling the air would make me lighter, and shuffled my way across the board.

Looking down made me dizzy. I had never been that high before. Even when I lived on the close, I never had a reason to go higher than the second floor. I knew now why my training included the bit on jumping from pillar to pillar — to get us used to leaping from rooftop to rooftop.

The board shifted some, making Vasilia wince. I froze in place and waited for it to snap, closing my eyes, too afraid to move.

"Now you're just being silly, Delmen," she said.

I felt her take hold of my hand and pull me toward her until I was on a roof again. I could breathe, now back on what amounted to more or less solid ground.

<<*Athletics Rank 3*>>

"I still don't understand why we had to come this way," I said.

"I told you already. After your theatrics in the gardens last night, guards are on high alert. Enforcers are patrolling the main roads like crazy. Even travelers are having trouble sneaking around."

She led me to the front end of the close where we were nearer to the ground level. "Not that I mind, you know. The less they're able to steal, the more there is for us."

We reached the ladder leading down to the landing one level above my flat. Vasilia went first. She sniffed at the air and checked for any sign of enforcers, but saw none. I was surprised they weren't keeping an eye on my flat or shop. If they intended to catch me, my home would be the place to watch.

"All clear," she whispered, waving me down the ladder. I landed with a thud loud enough to shake the floor. My thick work boots striking wood sent an echo down the close.

"Sorry," I whispered back. Aside from rolling her eyes at me, she didn't respond. When we rounded our way down the stairs to my level, I kept a lookout while she worked on unlocking the door, first trying my key and then tossing it to the ground after realizing the locks had been changed.

As she continued to work, I peered across Commercial Way to Meridia's empty shop. The door was still propped open. Bits of a scraped off decal still stuck to the window. Everything good about it was gone. I supposed I could no longer count it as one of my favorite places in Steamtown.

"All set." Vasilia interrupted my thoughts by swinging the old, creaking door open. As she did, our detection circles expanded. The magelight glyphs inside still functioned, pouring light out of my tiny flat into the close, illuminating us for the world to see. She pulled me inside and shut the door again before we were detected.

"You could have told me about the lights," she said.

"Sorry. I'm not used to thinking like a thief."

"You'd better learn quickly!" The tone in her voice was different than the woman I had come to know over the last few days, but I guess we were now 'on the clock,' in a way. She had little patience for screwing up when the consequences included getting caught.

I looked around the flat for any sign of entry. Aside from missing clothing and bedding, as far as I could see the room was just as I left it. I checked my closet first, finding nothing left for me. The clothes on my back and the shoes on my feet were all I had now.

I got to work on the floor as Vasilia circled the room.

"Can I take these?" she asked pointing at the glowing glyphs.

I nodded. She brought me here, so I thought she deserved some of the spoils for her efforts. She pocketed two of the three glyphs, leaving one out for light while I lifted the loose board and revealed my treasure box, a small jewelry chest containing a few dozen precious gems and a pouch of guilders I kept hidden for emergencies. I was pleased the box and its contents were intact and stuffed it into my inventory.

"Done?"

"Yeah, I'm done."

"Good. We have a long way to go to get to the High Mile. I suggest you stay close."

Keeping up with her was harder than I thought. She didn't offer me the same assistance as before, leaving me alone to climb ladders, sneak over planks carefully laid out or, in one instance, outright jumping over a narrow close.

As we moved, I had to cover my nose occasionally. Not all closes were created equal. Those with food vendors or pubs smelled particularly rancid. Crafter's Close was a paradise compared to some. It boiled down to the tolerance for filth of the residents living below us.

For the most part, Vasilia kept us closer to the lake-side of the alleyways we traversed, although whenever we got closer to Commercial Way, she took her time to remain as quiet as possible to avoid alerting guards patrolling below. And the guards did love to patrol. Between Crafter's Close and the gardens, I counted dozens of guards on the streets below oblivious to our passing overhead.

Aside from guards and enforcers, distinguished only by the color of their tabards, the streets were mostly deserted. Curfew was in effect, which meant all citizens were indoors. More savory travelers, those who visited Steamtown only for shops or quests, had no reason to be around. Just as I had no reason to leap from one rooftop to the next. I wasn't a thief. I was an enchanter.

Vasilia stopped ahead of me, perching at the edge of a building. She observed the close below, looking for any sign of guards while I waited patiently behind her, trying to catch my breath after our aerial dance down Commercial Way.

Garden Close was dark and empty, marked on one side by tenement houses. Opposite us, vendor stalls lined an iron fence that stretched the entire length of the garden from north to south. The only entrance I knew into the gardens was the main gate.

I spotted some torches at the gate, counting five guards standing at attention.

"They're looking for you," Vasilia said. "That ruckus you made last night triggered double lookouts."

"So how do we get by them? I don't have it in me to outrun that many guards. Not after last night."

"We'll have to distract them. There's no underground entrance leading to High Mile. At least none that I'm aware of." Vasilia began to climb down a ladder until she was standing one story above street level, only a few dozen feet from the gated entrance to the gardens. She held up a finger to ask me to wait as I started to climb down after her.

"You'll want to see this." She grinned at me before pulling out a small crossbow, hardly bigger than her head. I panicked as she loaded a dart into the device and aimed it at the guard closest to her.

"What are you doing? We can't attack them."

"Hush!"

Lining up her shot, she pulled the trigger. In an instant, her nameplate turned bright red. I suddenly feared her, feeling compelled to attack her with every ounce of strength in my body. I didn't know where the feeling came from, nor did I understand what inspired the wave of violent thoughts that filled my mind.

I did my best to suppress them, knowing Vasilia was my friend, and loosened the grip on my hammer. I didn't even realize I had drawn it. Her nameplate returned to green a few seconds later, and what she had done became apparent.

Where there were previously five guards with green nameplates, now one guard with a red nameplate lashed out at his green-plated comrades. A great frenzy overtook the guard like that of an animal. Whatever Vasilia did turned him into a rabid creature seeking to do as much damage as he could.

"Delmen, this won't last long," she whispered. Waving me after her, the two of us climbed down to the street, triggered stealth, and moved closer to the guards. As my detection ring approached them, the eye above me started to open. Right when I feared I would be detected, Vasilia reached into her pocket and pulled out a small pellet, throwing it to the ground.

The entire street filled with a dense fog, as though the thick haze that covered the lakes around Steamtown on most mornings was lifted up into the heights of the city. My eye icon, still visible through the fog, closed shut again. My detection ring shrank close to my body. I felt Vasilia's padded, paw-like hand grab me by the wrist as she sneaked me through the ruckus of confused guards.

I didn't struggle. I trusted her to get us to our destination. It was in her best interest and mine that we not be caught. Still, I felt uncomfortable not knowing where I was going. My feet, unable to find level ground, slipped along what were now tufts of soft grass. After what felt like an eternity of gliding through a thick haze, we stepped out of the mist and into the gardens.

The sound of fighting still echoed behind us. "How long are they going to fight one another?"

"Long enough for us to get to the other side."

"But won't they sound the alarm?" I asked.

"No. They won't know whether we entered or exited the garden. They will most likely feel too foolish to report the incident. Now stop asking questions! I didn't bring you with me to chat all night long."

She snarled at me, reminding me again that we were on the job. She wasn't my friend and bunkmate from the guild hall at this moment. Outside, she took her work seriously. I didn't doubt at all she would leave me behind to save herself.

When we reached the opposite end of the gardens, after sneaking by detection glyphs on the great lawn, I began to relax. While there were still guards patrolling the garden's central path, the opposite end leading to the High Mile was unattended. We crouched in some bushes to make sure we could exit the gardens safely.

"Looks like this'll be easier than I thought," Vasillia said. "The governor can step up patrols along Commercial Way all he wants, but he can't make more guards out of thin air."

She abandoned the bushes and beckoned me to follow. We mosied into High Mile district as effortlessly as two revelers out on an afternoon stroll. Once across, the fetid stench of Commercial Way began to fade. High Mile, unlike the rest of Steamtown, was clean. From what I heard, most residents could afford indoor plumbing. They didn't have to suffer showers of chamber pots and gardyloos all day long. Neither were they crammed in tenement-style quarters accessed only by a narrow, steep-sloped close.

That meant we couldn't climb rooftops or sneak down alleys. Instead, we rushed from one grand estate to the next, hiding as best we could from the few patrolling enforcers that passed us, none quite as alert as the patrols on Commercial Way.

After we passed ten estates, the governor's mansion and the queen's castle came into view. Moonlight reflected off the black-stained stone, reminding me that even the cleanest areas of the city still suffered from coal dust lingering in the air.

"Psst." Vasilia signaled me to get my attention. Crouching next to an iron gate, she pointed at our target — a three-story mansion edged with rose bushes. The house was grand, for sure, but not the most magnificent. A giant stoop led up to the front door that looked far too exposed to pick. I followed her as quietly as I could, a difficult task as I didn't know where I was going. I could barely see once we were beside the house.

Cloaked in shadow, I followed her behind the building. The view that met me was spectacular. A small private garden expanded away from the house to reach an abrupt end at a cliff. Beyond, the horizon went on forever. I saw hundreds of miles of forest, interrupted by the occasional glowing fire well beyond Steamtown's borders. For the first time in my life, I truly understood how much the city felt like a cage. I yearned like a captive creature to escape; only I knew nothing of the world beyond the city gates.

I spun around after I heard the creaking of a heavy door. Vasilia pocketed her lockpick and grinned. The house, now open to us, was silent. If anyone was inside, they seemed utterly oblivious to our trespassing. I climbed a smaller staircase behind Vasilia to follow her into the house. She stopped me with a firm palm on my chest.

"As I said, you can take anything you can carry. If you think something will make noise when you bother it, leave it alone. The last thing I need when I'm upstairs is for you to be bumbling about like a clumsy dwarf."

She moved into the house but then stopped before crossing the threshold. "And take off those damn boots." She chuckled a little before vanishing into shadow. A few moments later, barefooted, I joined her inside.

Magelight glyphs glowed on the wall, partially charged to serve more as nightlights rather than proper illumination. My detection circle encompassed most of the room I was in, a kitchen bigger than my old apartment.

The eye above me closed tight, like it was completely asleep, unconcerned that anyone should spot me. I looked around for loot to claim, ready to steal from someone else for the first time in my entire life. As I pulled open a drawer to find neatly stacked silverware, the fact that I was now a thief started to sink in. This was my life now. From vendor to thief after one act that cost Meridia and me dearly.

But I was determined to get my life back. And resolute in my desire to find Meridia and make things right for her. That drive encouraged me to stuff into my inventory as many polished pieces of silver as I could.

I didn't know the worth of silverware, but it didn't stop

me. I emptied the entire drawer one piece at a time, careful not to let them clink until half my inventory was full. Knowing kitchens, I had a hunch there was nothing left of value. What else could there be, save copper pots, porcelain plates, and other odds and ends? I made my way into an adjoining room, a dining area.

The table was human-sized, surrounded by a dozen chairs. In the middle, just out of my reach, two gold candlesticks beckoned me. I grabbed a chair and began to pull it into position, sure the prize would be worth the risk of making noise. The area rug under the table muffled the sound of the sliding chair, which creaked under my weight as I climbed onto it. The wood was sturdy, though, and allowed me to claim the candlesticks as my own. I took the half-burned candles, too.

Once on the floor, I wondered how long Vasilia would be. I heard no sounds of footsteps upstairs, but figured she was skilled enough to sneak without making a sound. I wasn't quite as skilled and discovered that the floor of the next room creaked wherever my foot fell. It made noise enough to remind me of Vasilia's warning, so I retreated into the dining room. The darkness of the room, absent even a most basic magelight glyph, combined with the sense of urgency I had to claim anything of value caused me to lose footing. In an instant, I caught my heel on the area rug and fell backward, my back pressing into the nearest chair.

The chair, taller than me, slid against my weight and banged into the table. I feared the noise would wake the home's inhabitants. I held my breath, waiting for a flurry of activity upstairs, worried they would catch Vasilia doing whatever she came here to do. I relaxed only after a minute passed, relieved that my clumsiness didn't give us away. Stepping away from the table, I peered back into the front room wondering what Vasilia was up to. What could she possibly be doing that would take so long? I thought about following her upstairs but ultimately decided not to, and backpedaled again, this time taking a wide berth around the table until I was in a room off to my right, an office.

Even when cast in shadows, I could tell the owner of this house was a person of worth. Stacks of papers littered the desk, scattered haphazardly with no method or system in place whatsoever. I squinted, looking for, as Horji put it, anything shiny. I spotted pens and wax sealers, inkwells, and magnifying glasses on the desk. The drawers could have offered some loot to take, but when I fumbled with my lock-pick to open them, a red X prevented me from picking the locks, followed by some text stating my skill level wasn't high enough.

Opposite the desk, the remains of a fire still burned in a small iron stove that heated the room. A flimsy-looking tea kettle swung on a hook above it. I approached and warmed my hands while I continued to scan the room. My feet also benefited from the warmth.

The stove, fixed atop a block of stone in the floor, radiated much-needed heat that was often hard to find in Steamtown. I stopped tending to myself when I spotted something I honestly thought would be a grand prize — two intricately decorated pistols affixed to weapons plaques on the wall. I crept across the floor, taking steps gentle enough to prevent any loud creaking until I reached the wall with the pistols. True enough, they were grand. Gold decorated the grips and barrels. A sheathed bayonet was affixed to the top of each gun, adding greater utility to the single-shot weapons. I had to steal them. Silver was good, but all the kitchen utensils in the world couldn't match the price of each pistol. Guns were always the most expensive thing to buy in Steamtown.

I stood on my toes trying to reach them, but they just rattled in place as my fingertips grazed the hilt. Needing something to stand on, I searched until I found a wooden crate next to the desk full of discarded paper. I emptied the box and turned it over, mulling over if it would hold my weight. I had to try. The heavy chair at the desk would make too much noise to drag over, and there was nothing else in the room to stand on. I took one step onto the crate, feeling the rough wood against the bottom of my feet. It buckled slightly but didn't budge. Using the wall to guide me up, I stepped with my other foot, making sure to stand on the edges of the box instead of in the middle.

I took a few deep breaths as the flimsy crate shifted some until I found my footing, before turning my attention back to the pistols. Removing them wasn't difficult. They weren't locked to the plaques. They rested on a single hook and two nails. The owner seemed to want to get at them quickly if he needed. I only relaxed once both were tucked safely in my inventory.

<<Sneak rank 7>>
<<Athletics rank 5>>

I took one step down to the floor. Before I reached it with my stubby legs, the box buckled violently as the wood gave way. I pushed off against the wall and closed my eyes tight knowing this would be the end. My fall would shake the house. The owner would wake up.

I didn't hit the ground, though. A set of firm arms caught me before I finished falling. Once upright, I realized it was Vasilia back from her adventure upstairs. I expected her to berate me for being too clumsy and noisy, but she only smiled. Taking hold of my wrist, she guided me outside. Once the door shut, we both breathed a sigh of relief, taking a moment to collect ourselves while I put my boots back on.

"Now that wasn't so bad, was it?" she whispered.

"Not so bad? I almost gave us away."

"But you didn't. That's why it's better to work in pairs."

"I still have a lot to learn, though."

"That you do. Now let's get out of here. We can take the exit in the gardens back to the lake. It'll save us some time."

I lamented the idea of getting in that stone coffin again, but it was better than sneaking our way back to Commercial Way, and some time along the water, however polluted, seemed like the perfect chance to unwind.

7

———

Hours later, we were back at the guild. Vasilia was kind enough to lead me to the guild vaults, a room secured by the most intricate locking mechanism I had ever seen. A giant wheel like the kind I'd seen in drawings of airships, required spinning in a specific order. Two keyholes needed to be unlocked before the wheel would turn. At a vendor stall next to the vault, a woman unlike any I had seen before sat with a pile of coins in front of her. I assumed this was Rasha, ready to purchase any pilfered items I secured that night.

As I approached, I got a closer look at her. She was a species I had never seen before. Her skin had the texture and appearance of tree bark. Instead of hair, a cascade of azure leaves flowed from her head, tied back and tucked behind her ears by vibrant green vines growing from her temples. Her eyes were familiar, though, like mine or Merrill's, more human than plant. She stared at me as I approached, and we locked gazes. The woman, if I could call her that, had a look about her that suggested she was not just old, but impossibly old, and unlike any other creature I had met before, she had no nameplate to identify her or her level.

We broke our mutual gaze when Vasilia interrupted us.

"Morning, Rasha," she said in a cheerful tone, as though she were speaking to her closest and dearest friend. It was a way I had never heard Vasilia talk to anyone before and wondered how she so readily adopted different personalities for different people, as though she was changing a mask. This may have been a trait shared by other Lycary, but I had no basis to compare her to. Any Lycary I had met before were travelers, and they made no sense to me.

"Morning, Vas. What do you have for me today?" Rasha formed what could best be called a smile, although she had no teeth to shape it. She spoke in a single tone and rhythm, emphasizing every syllable.

"Just the usual. I finished the plant job at the Grandach estate." Vasilia pulled out a wax seal stamp from her inventory and handed it to Rasha. The woman turned it over a few times, observing the crest on the bottom for authenticity, before collecting a handful of guilders and offering them to Vasilia. My half-wolf friend smiled and thanked the woman, patted me on the shoulder, and left without saying a word. She was too busy counting her coins as she walked away.

"And you, initiate. What do you have for me?"

"I'm afraid I don't have much," I said, pulling out the few dozen pieces of silverware, the gold-plated candlesticks, and the two pistols from my nearly packed inventory. I kept a hold of the gems. Their worth was not as individual minerals, but as carefully crafted glyphs. Each stone would sell for 20 pieces but would be worth almost a guilder when turned into a glyph, something I hoped to do once I returned to the common room.

I observed Rasha as she sorted through the objects. She grimaced a bit as she set aside the silverware. Lingering a moment on the candlesticks, she only formed a slight smile. Her attitude didn't make me feel very confident in my progress with the guild. She did lick her bottom lip a bit as she handled the pistols, first checking if they were loaded, then working the mechanics of them to make sure they worked. She gingerly set the guns aside as well, then got to counting from her pile of coins.

"Silver is too common. Don't bring me anymore unless it's jewelry," she instructed.

"I'm sorry, I didn't —"

"As for the candlesticks, the gold is good. It'll melt down nicely, but isn't worth much." I could tell she didn't want to be interrupted. "As for the guns. I can't sell them in Steamtown because of the crest on the hilt, but I can move them."

She thought a bit on the price. If it weren't for a sign nailed to the top of the stall reading "No Haggling" I might have asked for more. Instead, I felt satisfied with the 15 guilders and 50 pieces she handed me, even if each gun would sell for at least 15 in a shop. Recalling the price I owed the guild for paying my bounty, I did feel as though I was spinning my wheels. 5,000 guilders to gain my freedom seemed unobtainable. I turned to leave with my head held low, both in frustration and exhaustion after a long night of running, jumping, climbing, and sneaking.

"Wait a minute, initiate. We're not done."

"What do you mean?"

"Did no one tell you how guild ranks work?" she asked.

I shook my head. Merrill didn't volunteer the information, aside from a brief mention that I needed to earn my keep.

"Outside of petty theft, no one is going to trust you with guild assignments. While you're free to remain an initiate forever, you won't advance to Prowler until your account balance is 250 guilders, held in trust by me, the guild clerk. You can take your precious coins and leave at any time, or you can give them to me to hold in the vaults. Once you reach the total, you can talk to Merrill about promotion."

I felt like she was taking forever to get to the point. Each word was spoken between extended pauses, as though she struggled to form them. I considered her proposal, but I didn't yet know what price Vasilia would demand for information on Meridia and the Bean family.

"Thank you. I'll think about it," I said.

Rasha only nodded and turned her attention back to her coins, and to a thin notebook on the table where she jotted down the details of her job.

The way back to the common room took me by Merrill's quarters. His door was shut tight with no evidence he was in. Every other time I approached his room, light from his fireplace glimmered beneath the doorway. This time, his room appeared dark and quiet, signaling that he was either asleep or hadn't yet returned. I made my way to the common room, passing through the showers where a few guild members washed themselves off. Some of them were dirtier than others. Relatively clean myself, I entered the main hall looking for Vasilia. She was at her regular spot at the main table, dropping in a few coins to pay for the food she had already consumed. She looked about as beat as I was, and massaged her neck as I approached.

"You didn't do half bad for your first try," she said as I took a seat across from her, reaching across the table to claim a bit of bread and some cold meat.

"You think so?" I asked.

"Yeah. I mean you only would have gotten caught seven times if not for me, but that's not too shabby."

"How do you figure?"

"Well if you didn't take the rooftops, that's four times already, then there were the guards at the gardens, your bumping into that chair in the dining room, and your clumsy effort to steal those guns. If I hadn't already spiked the owner and his wife with sleeping powder, you'd most likely be in the stocks by now."

"Why didn't you tell me the owner wouldn't wake up?" I felt surprised, shocked, and a little amused.

"How would that have benefited you? You thought you

were taking a risk, and you acted accordingly. It helped you become a better thief."

"And what about you? You mentioned you did a plant job. What does that mean?"

"Plant jobs are the only job available for guild prowlers like me. It's all quite simple. Merrill has a list from the crow every week and some bit of 'evidence' of a mandate violation. We sneak in, plant the evidence, and get paid, usually more than what we would earn from thieving alone."

"But wouldn't these folks end up in the stockades if caught?"

"Not necessarily. My guess is it's usually one rival or another in High Mile hoping they'll get reassigned back to a commoner's life. I've never heard of an aristocrat getting sent to the stocks. The governor treats his upper class well. They're the ones who pay his salary."

I thought I was starting to get the hang of the guild. It seemed they didn't want to be responsible for harming anyone. The person I robbed wouldn't miss the items I stole. The guns, perhaps, but not the silverware and candlesticks. I turned my attention back to Vasilia and started to ask another question, about the information I wanted on Meridia, but she interrupted me with a silent yawn.

"I know what you're going to ask. My price is fifteen guilders. Pony up the money and I'll tell you everything I've learned about your friend."

I nodded. I could earn a little over five more guilders, for sure. It just meant spending the next day crafting glyphs instead of stalking the streets. Soon enough, I finished eating and cleaned myself, only I wasn't tired anymore. The prospect of helping Meridia kept me wide awake. I left to explore the guild, heading back to Rasha's stall, hoping she could point me in the direction of the closest enchanter's bench.

Rasha wasn't as forthcoming as I would have hoped, but after promising her one of my glyphs, she relented and pointed me down the left path near the washroom, opposite Merrill's quarters. The tunnel split and bent like a river, but I "kept to the left" as she told me. Eventually, after I feared I had gone too far, I found the crafting room. It suffered from an immense level of disuse with magelight glyphs on the wall dull and dark from lack of charging.

I channeled some of my mana into the glyph and the room, in a disordered state of disrepair, lit up. I had to climb over piles of discarded and broken furniture before reaching the enchanter's bench. After wiping a thick layer of grime off it with my sleeve, I got to work polishing the stones, coating them with glow dust paste from my inventory, and etching into them the runes required to channel power. I felt like myself again. Creating enchanting glyphs was always thera-peutic for me. I took pride in doing something that shaped a product others could enjoy. I often felt I was born to be a crafter but had no knowledge of my parents or my past to suggest it was what I was meant to do.

I wasn't born to be a thief. That was clear. I didn't think anyone was, but if anybody proved me wrong, it would be Merrill and Horji, who both seemed born for this life.

I got to thinking about my limitations as an enchanter. No longer subject to mandates, I could improve my craft. All I had to do was find new rune patterns, which meant I needed to either break into another enchanter's shop — against the guild rules — or purchase higher-level glyphs to study. I would hardly make bank on armor improvement, weapon damage enhancement, or magelight glyphs. I could perhaps learn glyphs unique to thieving and sell them on the side here, skipping Rasha entirely.

As I finished the first glyph, a stoneskin enchantment made of a single opal, I thought about how to secure materi-als. I only had so much glow dust for my limited stock of gems. On Commercial Way, I would pop off to a jewelry vendor and purchase the gems I needed from her. I couldn't do that now. The city during the day was no place for me. With no shadows to hide in, the enforcers would catch me for sure.

I pocketed the glyph and began working on a second, this one a weapon enchantment. As I etched glyph after glyph, I lost track of time. I focused on the last week and a half and all that had happened to me, remembered fond dinners out with Meridia, and worried about what happened to her. It wasn't until I heard my name when I lost focus, nearly shattering a gem.

"Delmen, what are you doing?" Merrill stood in the doorway. He was dirty. Dirtier than I had seen anyone before, covered from head to toe in muck.

"I'm crafting glyphs. What does it look like?"

"It looks like someone who isn't interested in becoming a better thief. Why aren't you asleep? Sunset is in two hours. If you don't partner up when everyone wakes up, you'll be on your own tonight, and you're not ready to be on your own."

"I'm not going out there tonight. I can make more turning these gems into glyphs than I can from stealing. Anyhow, what's one missed night when compared to the information Vasilia will sell to me?"

"You're still on about the Bean family, aren't you?" He moved into the room, kicking aside broken chairs to get closer to me. As he did, I spotted a deep gash across his face, stretching from his right brow to his left cheek. It seemed he had a hard go of whatever job he tried to do last night.

"Yes. You don't understand. I can't just do nothing. I need to find out what happened. If I can save Meridia, I must try."

"You do know it's hopeless, don't you? If the Beans snatched her, nothing you can do will win her freedom. No one comes back from—"

He stopped speaking before he revealed their location to me. "No. I won't help you with this at all. I offered you a chance to become something great. You have the potential to be a very skilled thief. If you want to throw it away by following this path, that's your choice. I've given you too much attention already."

He turned around to leave but stopped to say one more thing. "As promised, your guild armor is in the common room for you. You'll find it better than the clothes you're currently wearing, especially the boots."

"I don't understand your faith in me. I'm nothing special. I'm just a clumsy dwarf."

"And Horji was just a clumsy gnome. As with most things in life, skill comes with practice. In my experience, the best thieves in the guild started out just like you. In time, I don't see why you couldn't become one of the highest ranking members in our little guild. You have the work ethic. You just need to figure out if that's something you want."

He didn't wait for me to respond, leaving before I could think his words over. I replayed his last statement in my mind a few times as I polished a garnet with some glow dust. I didn't linger too long on the conversation, though. I knew the answer quickly enough. I wasn't born for this life. I didn't want to survive forever at the expense of others. My job was to increase my guild rank, pay off my bounty, and, then get my life back. And that meant finding a way to earn 5,000 guilders.

I started to work on the garnet but was struck by how tired I was. Halfway through the box of gems I saved from my flat, I knew when to call it quits. The last thing I needed was to destroy one of my few remaining jewels because I was too tired to pay attention. With eleven glyphs finished, I headed back to Rasha's stall hoping she would still be around. As I approached, it was quite clear that her job required she work in reverse. Where we were asleep all day and up all night, she seemed to be on a regular cycle. She was already packing things up when I approached and groaned at me for interrupting the end of her business day.

Without saying a word, I plopped the finished glyphs down on her table. She eyed them all carefully with half a smile, pocketing one as the price for her help earlier, and handed me five guilders and 25 pieces for the remaining ten. I accepted her price, although I knew I could sell them myself for twice as much, and rushed back to the common room in time to catch Vasilia and the others waking up. While everyone else ignored me, Vasilia eyed me shadily. "Where have you been all night? You look like crap."

"I've been busy," I said as I took out the fifteen guilders I owed her for information.

She counted the coins with a look of surprise on her face. "So be it. I'll tell you what I've found out in the morning. I'd ask you to come with me again tonight, but you look like you're going to pass out. Get some sleep. I'll be back in a few hours."

"Isn't there anything you can tell me now?" I was impatient. And part of me didn't wholly trust Vasilia to give me all the information I needed. I'd only known her a few days.

"Don't worry. You'll get all the information and more when I get back. I didn't expect you to come up with the money so quickly. I'm still waiting for a report from one of my contacts. We'll talk when I return."

I nodded at her, thinking it best not to press her any further. Exhausted, I stumbled over to my bed where I found armor waiting for me: dark leather pants, boots, gloves, a belt, and a leather cuirass as Merrill promised. The worn hide was soft but dull. I rotated the chest piece around and noticed it didn't reflect any light, where standard leather goods were polished until they shone. This, though, appeared to be treated with a sand scrub. I appreciated the attention to detail. It would help me to hide better if any source of light didn't make me shine like a beacon.

Setting the gear aside, I crawled into bed and pulled the blanket over my head. It took me a while to get tired again.

Anxiety about what Vasilia would tell me in a few hours paired with the flurry of activity going on around me made sleeping difficult. I traced in my mind the path Vasilia took me on that night, from the tunnel we took to South Bridge, to the way up to the rooftops, to sneaking our way through the gardens. She even had the patrol path of the detection glyphs memorized. I knew I had my work cut out for me. Vasilia, only a prowler with the guild, was a substantially better thief than I was. It was odd that she hadn't yet ranked up, but for now that was a question for another day.

8

___

"Come with me." I woke up violently, shock shuddering through my body. At some point in the night, I managed to shed my dirty shirt. My blanket was knotted around me.

Vasilia stood over me, an impatient and tired air about her. She didn't look pleased. Maybe she had a lousy night outside.

"Come on, Delmen, get up." She grabbed me and pulled me out of bed. I found my shirt in a bundle on the floor, next to a heap of armor that made up my guild set. I grabbed everything and shoved it in my inventory, yanking on my shirt as she pulled me behind her.

She was the first one back. We passed Merrill's quarters. I saw a light flicker under the door suggesting he was around.

Is this it? Does she have the information I need?

I struggled to keep up with her, especially as she pulled me into unfamiliar tunnels I had never seen before. She slipped through one narrow passageway after the next, leaving me trying to squeeze my broad torso through. Whenever I thought I might lose her, she stopped and waited for me to catch up.

"Hurry up. You're slow, like a baby," she said. She revealed her incisors, smiling.

Lycary are so hard to read.

Down and down we went, deeper into the mountain where the black tiles of the guild gave way to rough rock, dry support beams, and signs of long-abandoned mining activity. Where was she leading me, why did she need to take me so far away to give me the information?

My frustration mounted when it became too hard for me to see. Magelight glyphs became sporadic. Remnants of tallow lights stuck to the wall, none brightening our way. When I was fed up after thirty minutes of chasing her and was about to ask her to explain herself, she stopped.

"We're here," she said.

I didn't know what she meant. We were at a dead end with no visible egress, but Vasilia drew a dagger from her belt, and with the tip of the blade she tapped the wall blocking our way in a combination-like pattern. The tunnel trembled. The door slid into the earth, a triggered mechanism lowering it down. Sunlight cascaded into the tunnel. I raised my hand to block the light, finding it hard to open my eyes.

Being blind didn't stop Vasilia from pulling me out of the tunnel into the open. I panicked, worried that exposure during the day would result in being captured by the guards, but when I was able to see again, I found I wasn't in Steamtown at all. Instead, I was standing near the shore of a large island on the lake north of the city. We had traversed caves and mines that went under the lake.

"Why did you bring me here?" I asked Vasilia.

"Because you paid me for information, and here is where the information will lead you."

"What do you mean?"

"I heard back from my contacts a few hours ago. I'm not certain how, but they were able to confirm that Sawney Bean took your friend. After you killed that traveler, her landlord kicked her out. After the guards fined her for mandate viola-tion, she didn't have enough money for even the common house. Since she hasn't resurrected at Steamtown Cemetery, we can only conclude that the Bean family still holds her in their lair. And their lair is here."

She pointed away from the shore, toward the center of the island. There, a hill a quarter the size of the moun-tain holding Steamtown reached into the sky. At the bottom of the mound, I saw a massive stone obelisk, four times my height and as wide as a horse. Behind it and up a winding path, a wooden door revealed the entrance to a mine shaft. Although there were no guards in sight, there were plenty of people, all travelers, save a single citizen staffing a rickety vendor stall opposite the obelisk.

"You still haven't told me who the Beans are," I said.

"Are you sure you want to know?"

I nodded. It was up to me to rescue Meridia. To do that, I needed as much information as possible.

"Very well," she said. She sighed while scratching behind her ear. I sensed she didn't want to tell me, but I needed to know.

"Remember when Merrill explained to you the various factions in Dark Market? There's the thieves guild, the assas-sins guild, the mercantile guild, a necromancers guild, and countless other factions of snatchers."

"What are snatchers?" I asked.

"They're precisely what they sound like. Their goal is to profit off the capture and use of other citizens. Some snatchers hold citizens for ransom. Some sell those they catch into slav-ery. Some use them for food. Some sell them to the necro-mancers, which is why we stay clear of them. The Bean clan, some forty to fifty strong, are the most notorious group of snatchers in the region. No one knows why they kidnap people. They don't sell them as slaves. They don't talk to any other guilds or factions. And they don't demand a ransom for those taken.

"All we know is they take without warning, without mercy, and always bring their captives to their lair, to this place. No one has ever come out of there after being taken. The only folks who dare enter are travelers. Even then, only in groups of four or more. Many end up resurrecting at the graveyard less than an hour later. From what we've learned, this place makes the stockades look like a spa."

While she explained the situation to me, I observed the scene. Scores of travelers waited near the obelisk. Some joined together and focused on the stone pillar until, a few moments later, another traveler appeared. Multiple groups lingered for a while waiting for others to join them. This led to a steady stream of groups entering the lair, all seemingly ready and eager for conflict.

"This is why Merrill didn't want to tell you. If you go in there, you might as well kiss your freedom goodbye. You'll either get snatched or killed. Either way, you'll end up in there for the rest of your life or captured and reassigned to the stocks. If you decide to go in, you're on your own." She never sounded so somber. I'd seen her frustrated, gleeful, friendly, arrogant, and pointed. Now, though, she was dark. She didn't want me to go in there, but I knew I had to.

I couldn't live with myself if Meridia, my only real friend, was trapped in that place the rest of her life. I had to find a way to save her. And if no citizen was willing to help me, then I knew what I had to do.

"Perhaps I won't be on my own, after all," I said to her. "If none from the guild will help, perhaps the travelers will."

"You're welcome to try, but if I've learned anything, it's that travelers help no one. At least not without a reward. What could you possibly offer them that would get them to help you?"

"I don't know, but I have to try."

Vasilia became quiet again. She turned toward me and looked me straight in the eyes. "Please, Delmen, don't."

I didn't know how to respond. I didn't want to make her sad. At the same time, I refused to abandon Meridia. My freedom meant nothing if it came at the cost of a friend's suffering.

"Thank you," I said. "For everything."

I left Vasilia's side and strode with confidence over to the obelisk, even though being surrounded by travelers made my skin crawl. They represented the worst Steamtown had to offer. They were killers, thieves, and rowdy revelers. They were vile bastards, the lot of them, and would sooner kill me than help me, but I had to try.

Standing at the bottom of the path leading to the Bean lair, I asked each group passing by for help.

"Please, I need your help to rescue my friend," I said. Some groups laughed at me as they passed. Others ignored me completely. Across the open field, I caught Vasilia watching me for a few minutes before she left. The stone door leading back into the underground closed shut, leaving a red crystal in the ground I recognized as my way back into the guild. I felt comfortable knowing I could return if I wanted, but was resolute that someone would help me. Someone had to have heart enough to help, even if I had nothing to offer in return.

The stream of travelers continued to pass by for hours. The sun was high in the sky, near noon, by the time the groups slowed down. While most continued to ignore me, some threatened me. I chose to retreat when those people were around, hiding nearby the vendor stall. The vendor, a citizen human, refused to talk to me when he read my bounty. He warned me that he'd call the guards if I came any closer, so I kept my distance.

An hour later, just as I had started getting hungry, I thought about returning to the guild hall and coming back another day. I tried one last group of travelers, led by a female Wulver, a level 14 named Bunny Boo. As much as I was curious about her odd name, I wondered more what distinguished her from a Lycary. As she approached, I realized. While Lycary were very wolf-like, Wulvers appeared more like domestic dogs, with floppy ears and more formed snouts. She was with an already formed party of an elf, a dwarf in heavy armor, and a gnome.

"Please," I asked her as she walked by. "I need your help."

She looked at me. For the first time in over six hours, a traveler looked at me. She didn't ignore me. She didn't threaten me, and she didn't laugh at me. Instead, she responded with empathy.

"What do you need?" she asked. Her voice was kind but impatient.

"I need your help. The Bean clan captured my friend. I need to rescue her."

Her companions chimed in, all questioning me about rewards for helping. They weren't as pleasant as her. One, a level 12 elf named Brunar, scoffed. The other two, a gnome named Fizzlestick and a dwarf named Rumper, dismissed me completely.

"Bunny, he's not worth it. He doesn't even have a quest. This looks like some pointless role-playing shit," Brunar said. I didn't understand his words.

"You don't know that. We've run this place over twenty times, and we've never seen him before. Maybe he's a hidden quest. I say we bring him with us."

"Fine, but if he does anything stupid or slows us down, I'll stop healing him."

They whispered among themselves how best to proceed, before agreeing that it was worth it to them to bring me into the lair. A second later, an option popped up in my field of vision.

<<Bunny Boo has invited you to a group. Do you accept?>>

The moment I focused on the accept option, something strange happened. Text exploded in my field of view, flickering like a magelight glyph almost out of mana. I couldn't understand what was happening to me, but what I saw changed dramatically. It was as though the world shattered, to be put back together in an unfamiliar way. When I looked down, I saw a set of boxes, one containing my hammer. I focused on it, and my mallet instantly appeared in my hand. I opened up my inventory bag and concentrated on my guild armor pieces, and they immediately materialized on my body. I didn't need to change into them.

To the top right, I saw my picture and a set of colored bars next to it, red, green, and blue. And to the left, a circle that I thought held a map of the region. Lastly, and most curiously, I saw matching portraits of the travelers, all with their own red, green, and blue bars. I didn't know what to make of it. Was this how travelers viewed the world, with all of this added information to help them? Why did they get additional interface options we citizens didn't have?

"Hurry up before we leave you behind!" I heard Brunar say. Bunny smiled at me and motioned for me to go ahead of her. My heart skipped a beat as we approached the entrance to the lair. I felt a sense of foreboding as the doors creaked open upon our approach, and my resolve wavered for the first time since I discovered Meridia's fate. Behind the doors, a shimmering portal waited. I couldn't see beyond it, but as Rumper, Fizzlestick, and Brunar stepped in, I knew if I didn't follow, I would lose my only chance.

With a lump in my throat, I clenched my hammer and stepped through. For a moment, I felt the same sense of self-aware oblivion that I felt last time I was killed. This didn't last long. The world that had faded from view reappeared again. Behind me, the doors to the outside were shut and blocked by the very same portal I stepped through. Ahead of me a slime-coated tunnel sunk deep into the ground. There was no other way but down.

<<Delmen MacDougall zoned to Bean Clan Mines>>

"Delmen, do you know where your friend is?" Bunny asked me.

"I've never been here before. She could be anywhere."

"No problem. We're going to try to clear the entire place anyhow. If she's here, we'll find her."

I heard the sound of a blade unsheathing. Rumper, at the front of the group, raised his sword and shield as he moved down the tunnel. He turned to the others. "Where do you want to go first?" he asked.

Having not heard him speak before, I suppressed a laugh. I expected a rough-sounding dwarf warrior. Instead, I listened to a voice more like a child. Every few words he spoke carried with it the cracking sound a boy makes when he starts his growth.

"How about Burke and Hare? It's the closest, and one of the easiest fights. It'll be a nice warm-up," Bunny said.

Warm up? They're acting like this is some game.

"That'll bring us through the plague halls. We can save some cure disease potions if we go around and hit the Torturer first, then take the boat over to the laboratory," Rumper said.

Bunny shrugged, and the group decided, following him further into the lair. I had no idea how they knew so much about this place, unable to imagine why anyone would come in here willingly, but travelers flowed in like this was a food market.

I followed them in the middle of the pack, with Bunny and Brunar behind me. As we walked deeper and deeper into the lair, the air grew damp and more rancid, like the smell of Crafter's Close after a prolonged drought. I expected the tunnel to become darker as we delved further, but was perplexed to find uniform lighting with no source of illumination in sight. There were no magelight glyphs, no torches, no tallow lights. The air glowed to light our way. It all felt very artificial, like porcelain fruit or paper flowers.

"Meridia, where are you," I whispered to myself.

"Who's Meridia? Is that your friend?" Bunny asked me.

"She's my only friend, and she's here because of me."

"Why? What did you do?"

"A traveler assaulted her in her shop. I attacked and killed him, then ran away like a coward. She lost her home. With nowhere to go, the Beans captured her."

"Well, that would explain the bounty, but not why she was kicked out. She was the victim, right?" Bunny asked. Her attitude toward me changed when I mentioned my attacking the traveler.

"It doesn't matter when your kind is involved. If we take one step out of line, or if we dare violate a single one of our mandates, we can lose everything."

She stepped back and whispered to Brunar something about never hearing an NPC talk like me. Both of them eyed me suspiciously. She was going to ask another question when Rumper, at the front of the group, shushed us. We reached a split in the tunnel, right leading up further into the hillside and left extending down, most likely under the lake. I followed him down to the left where the passageway quickly turned into an open room, a prison. From the far end of the hall, I could hear screams of agony — the sounds of multiple torture victims.

"Same as last time," Brunar said. "Don't stop until we reach the torture chamber."

As we filed into the room, an iron gate behind us dropped with a bang, blocking our way out and alerting whoever was around to our presence. The hairs on my arm stood on end. Screaming became louder and madder, fueled by insanity.

Instinctively, I activated stealth. Unlike when I was sneaking in Steamtown, here I was almost translucent. Despite the others surrounding me, the eye icon didn't register their presence. They didn't have any detection circles.

"So he's a rogue," Bunny said. "I wondered what class he might be."

She was interrupted by the sound of squealing hinges. One of the prison cells opened, its door cracking into the wall, and some citizens rushed out, their nameplates glowing bright red. I stepped back as one ran by me, straight for Brunar, who screamed and banged his sword into his shield to draw their attention.

None of them had any weapons. Some didn't even have all their limbs. They scratched at his armor while Bunny and Fizzlestick attacked, Bunny with spells and Fizzle with a rifle. I nearly jumped as a wolf appeared next to the gnome. It rushed by me, lunging at a nearby enraged citizen. The weight of the creature as it passed me caused me to backstep, breaking my stealth. I was now visible to the citizens. One, a level 9 human woman, clawed at me with fingers that looked worn down to the bone.

Acting on instinct, I swung my hammer and struck her in the head, dazing her. She whimpered like an injured dog and retreated into the cell. Bunny grabbed my arm and pulled me after her. As we pressed further into the room, more cells violently opened. More crazed citizens rushed out to fight us. I didn't know what to think. I had to fight them. They were trying to kill me. I couldn't imagine the torture that turned them into such violent beasts.

As we approached the end of the room, I looked back at a heap of corpses on the floor, some dismembered by Rumper, some smoldering with the remnants of fire from Bunny's fire spells, and some gunshot wounds marked on their bodies after Fizzle shot them down. A few, I had to admit, had their skulls cracked open by my hammer.

As we exited the room through a decaying archway, a door slammed shut. Bunny and Brunar charged the door and lowered a metal bar to lock it in place just as a wave of enraged prisoners crashed into it. The force of the impact sent both of them back a few feet where they stood with wide, maniacal grins.

<<Light armor Rank 2>>
<<One-handed Rank 3>>

I heaved, trying to catch my breath. "What was wrong with them?" I asked the group.

They all turned to me with a look that suggested they forgot I was there.

"What do you mean? They're beserkers. They're always like that. Gives us something to kill between boss fights."

I became angry, thinking that Meridia or any of my fellow citizens snatched by the Beans could end up like this. "Those people are citizens of Steamtown, not fodder for you to kill for enjoyment!"

"Bunny, I'm growing tired of this. Seems like he's only here for those who want to role-play. Let's ditch him," Brunar said.

"No! I want to see how his story plays out. Plus he held his own back there just fine. Let's get on with this. I have to sign off in an hour."

There it was again. Strange terms and concepts I didn't understand. I'd never talked to travelers this intimately before. From what I could tell, they acted like what they were doing didn't matter to them, like coming in here was something they did for fun. I didn't dare ask any more questions. Bunny was the only one among them wanting me around. I didn't want to press my luck and risk them turning against me.

We continued, now down a spiral staircase with torches affixed to the wall. They glowed green, unlike any fire I had seen. The flames cast an eerie shadow down the underground mine shaft. As we descended, tortured screams grew louder and louder. It took all my willpower not to cover my ears. I had never heard such agony before. The others didn't seem fazed by it at all, and my anger toward them amplified as a result. How could they not be saddened by others suffering?

We reached the bottom of the underground shaft. Another doorway opened into a room full of strange instruments and contraptions. Dozens of citizens were present, alive, and enraged, although they didn't rush us. They couldn't. Some were secured to inverted tables, hanging from their ankles. Others were tied to a contraption that stretched their limbs. I spotted a female citizen, a human, strapped to a chair made of iron spikes, a small fire burning under the chair to heat it up and scorch her flesh. They all seemed barely alive.

As I walked by a set of large cages hanging from the ceiling, I felt Bunny pull me back just as a man lashed out at me. I could see every bit of him. Naked and shivering, the man didn't have an ounce of fat or muscle on him. His guttural scream startled me. The horror around me left me dizzy and nauseous.

I searched for Meridia amongst the torture victims but saw no sign of her. There wasn't a single elf in the room. I continued my search, passing by Rumper. The four of them yelled at me to stop. I listened, just before reaching the center of the room, an unobstructed area with no instruments, no contraptions, and no tortured souls. It looked more like an arena, with a single table in the middle. Standing at the table, his back to us, a hulk of a man worked a cleaver on a slab of unidentifiable meat. He didn't seem to notice we were there.

Rumper grabbed me by the collar and launched me backward. I skidded across the floor a few feet, jagged stone ripping at my hands. "You almost triggered the boss, you idiot!"

Bunny helped me to my feet. "Rump, calm down. He's an

NPC. He doesn't understand. Let's get on with it. I have to sign off soon."

"All right, but if he gets in the way, I'm not saving him."

Bunny turned to me. "Just stay by my side. If anything attacks me, you can handle it. Don't try to attack the Torturer unless we tell you."

I nodded. I was confused, but if she instructed me to stick to her like glue, I was going to. I watched as they all prepared for a fight, puzzled about why attacking a single man armed with a kitchen utensil made them so tense. Standing behind and to the side of Bunny, I watched as Rumper raised his sword and shield. He charged the Torturer, a nameless level 12 human nearly twice as tall as me.

The Torturer responded to Rumper's charge and spun around, catching his sword just in time. With his free hand, he swung his other arm, holding a second meat cleaver, which crashed into Rumper's shield. The dwarf's red bar and green bar flickered and shrank. Brunar, next to me, raised his hand and a bolt of golden light erupted from his palm, whistled across the room, and struck Rumper in the back. His red bar, I deduced to be his overall health, increased back to full. Brunar's blue bar reduced by an appropriate amount before it slowly started to rise again, although I didn't understand how.

The Torturer roared like a lion, swinging both his cleavers in a giant arc that pierced the air. I felt a hand on top of my head push me down just in time to avoid a red beam that shot across the room, slicing in half anything that got in its way.

"Duck every time he does that," Bunny told me. She stood back up and stepped closer to the Torturer with surprising agility. When I first saw her puppy-dog like face, I half expected she would be clumsy. Raising her staff, she focused. At the same time, flames erupted from the Torturer's skin, and her blue mana bar reduced.

Fizzlestick was also occupied, unleashing bullet after

bullet at the man they battled. Fixated on them, I barely spotted the Torturer break free from Rumper's focus. With his thick leg, he kicked at the dwarf and sent him tumbling. The human stared at me, rage in his eyes, and started a fast walk toward me. A red skull appeared above my head. I knew I was in trouble.

"Delmen, run!" I heard someone yell. It wasn't Bunny, it was one of the guys. I backpedaled a few steps, almost tripping over myself. My thin-soled boots still tripped me up. I managed to stay on my feet, running in time to avoid the bite of the Torturer's cleaver. He continued to chase me for what felt like forever, although I knew it was less than a minute. I had to duck twice to avoid his swinging cleavers that damaged everything in the room. The red skull over my head blinked a few times before disappearing, and the man turned his attention away from me and back to Rumper, ready for him in the center of the room.

"All right, hit him from behind!" Bunny yelled.

"What are you doing? We don't need an NPC to fight!" Brunar snapped at Bunny, but she ignored him.

"Just do it. Use your hammer."

Every ounce of me didn't want to strike him. Flashes of that night in Meridia's shop appeared in full color in my mind, as though it only happened a few hours before, but I realized if I was going to survive this place, if I was going to find her, I needed to be less like myself, less like a passive citizen, and more like a traveler.

I gripped my hammer as tightly as I could. The hilt, slick with my sweat, was hard to hold onto, but it didn't stop me from swinging it over my head and striking the Torturer as high as I could reach. My hammer hit him just above his hips, in the small of his back. He didn't seem to register any pain.

I followed him, swinging with every ounce of energy I had, releasing all of my built up rage and frustration. My green bar reduced with every swing until I reached the middle of the room. I tried for one more hit but couldn't raise my weapon. Even my feet refused to budge. This lasted a few moments until the bar replenished. The Torturer now battled Rumper while the others continued their onslaught, Fizzlestick with bullets, Bunny with fire spells, and Brunar with what I determined to be healing magic to keep us all alive.

I ducked to avoid another disc of energy produced by the Torturer's knives. Bunny released one final spell before the man enraged. He roared. All the other citizens tied to their various contraptions matched his roar in unison. Their shackles came undone. One by one, they fell to the floor and started crawling toward us, reaching out with their gnarled, knobby fingers. I estimated there were forty of them closing in on us. I found myself uttering a small prayer of protection to both Braka and Noctra at the same time, swinging my hammer at the nearest citizen who stretched his arms out at me.

I glimpsed in him a tortured soul, a fellow dwarf. He looked so familiar, as though I was staring at myself in a mirror. When his hand grazed my leg, our locked stare broke. Pain jolted up from the spot he touched me. My red bar reduced substantially, quickly mitigated by a salvo of healing magic Brunar infused in the entire group. He clapped both his hands together for a few moments before separating them, releasing a golden haze of light.

Then it all stopped. The screams of his victims, the Torturer's roar, the sound of metal clashing on metal, and the zing of spells soaring through the air ceased. The dwarf citizen clawing at me collapsed into a dead heap, then crumbled to dust, leaving nothing behind but a crumbling pile of bones on the floor.

<<One-handed rank 4>>
<<One-handed rank 5>>
<<Athletics rank 6>>

<<Light armor rank 3>>
<<You have defeated the Torturer - level 12>>
<<Reward: 10 guilders>>
<<Reward: Steel meat cleaver, 7 damage>>
<<Reward: Steamtown reputation +25>>

The text vanished before I could read most of it. I heard the clink of objects and coin dropping into my inventory, and wondered about the label I saw over the cleaver when I focused on it. Curious, I put my hammer in my bag and concentrated on that as well.

<<Mana-infused Crafter's Hammer. 9 damage>>

"What's going on? Why was he so hard to kill?" I asked Bunny. She stood next to me drinking a flask of water. The more she swallowed, the faster her blue bar refilled.

"He was a boss, the second hardest in the dungeon. You did well, though. For an NPC, that is."

I felt emboldened. I heard the term NPC used too many times. "What's an NPC?"

Brunar hushed Bunny before she answered and pulled her aside to talk to her. They were talking about me.

"Why won't any of you ever answer my questions? What are NPCs? What are these strange bars and symbols I'm seeing? Even when I close my eyes, I can see them!"

Rumper walked over from the middle of the room where the Torturer's corpse still occupied the floor. "You think he's a glitch?" he asked the others.

Bunny shrugged. "Must be. Maybe he's a new feature from the last patch. Who knows. I'm curious to see how his story plays out, though. Let's keep going."

"Why won't you answer me?" I yelled. I was becoming furious. My anger toward travelers was building up within me.

"Because! We. Don't Want. To! If you have a problem with that, you can leave," Rumper yelled back at me. "Seriously, we have less than an hour before we have to go. If you want to find your precious friend, stop slowing us down."

I had pressed my luck and lost. A few deep breaths later, I was calm enough to continue, so followed after them as they exited the torture room into a narrow tunnel. I didn't trust them, though, so I drew my hammer for good measure. If they decided to turn on me, I would try to give them a fight.

We continued for a few minutes until the stink of the torture chamber faded. The air grew colder, damper, but smelled fresh, like water in the fountain at the Royal Gardens. And I heard water running as well. The roaring sound of a fast-moving river echoed down the corridor. The tunnel widened. The wall to my left ended, leaving one side of the path edging an underground river, its water so black I couldn't see the current.

We continued until we reached a dock where a small boat bobbed back and forth, ropes tightened by the force of the river trying to carry it away.

"All aboard!" Bunny said. She seemed giddy, happier than she should have been in a place like this. Where I first thought her the kindest traveler I met, I realized she was just like the rest of them.

I struggled to get onto the boat, my legs too short to reach across the gap. I started to fall when Brunar and Rumper caught me and pulled me into the vessel. They both chuckled as I spun over, landing on the floor with a loud thud. As I tried to get up, Rumper pushed me down with his steel boot. "Stay down there. Trust me."

He pulled out his sword and hacked at the ropes, freeing the boat from the dock. We lurched forward, guided by the current until we disappeared into a tunnel as dark as midnight during a new moon. Despite the darkness, I could still make out every detail of the others. Fizzle held onto the oar guiding the rudder. Rumper held his shield up to protect Bunny while Brunar held her legs in place. She looked like she was preparing for an attack.

I peeked over the gunwale but saw nothing. All I could make out were the swaying sandbags attached to the hull to soften the shock taken every time the boat crashed into the sides of the cave. I heard a chattering, though, like the sound swarming rats made. I fell back when I felt something strike my face. Touching my cheek with my fingers, I felt blood.

"Now, Bunny!" one of the others yelled.

I looked up and saw Bunny raise her staff into the air. From the tip, a torrent of fire shot out to fill the entire channel ahead of us. Her mana bar dropped precipitously. Meanwhile, Brunar cast his own spell. A blue stream connected the two of them. As his mana lowered, hers began to climb. Corpses of roasted creatures crashed into the boat, all killed after flying through her flame wall. They were bats, hundreds of them, and they looked mutated — the largest bats I had ever seen. One landed with a thud between my legs and lashed out at me. I smashed it with my hammer, killing the vile creature without a second thought. I heard Rumper chuckle at my panicked response.

This went on for the better part of a minute before the shrieking sounds of bats faded and the boat, violently bobbing on the current, slowed. It gently floated down the river. When it reduced to a near crawl, Brunar and Fizzle jumped over the edge and onto another dock, where they tethered the vessel in place. I joined the others, this time finding it easier to get off the boat. We were outside a broad set of doors, similar to those guarding the thieves guild's main entrance. The symbol of Noctra was carved into one door. On the other, I saw a glowing red outline of a healer's crest, a heart with a spiral embedded in the middle.

A sign staked outside the doors read "Burke and Hare Incorporated."

"If we're going to find your friend, she may be in here. Burke and Hare are snatchers. They've even tried to take some of us on occasion," Bunny said. She approached the doors and traced the tip of her staff along the spiral symbol. A few clicks and the grinding of gears drove the door open, revealing a black-tiled room. This tile wasn't polished like in the thieves guild. It was stained, worn from decades of neglect. The tiles shattered under my feet as we moved down the hallway.

"Guys," Bunny said, "I don't have a whole lot of time. Can we skip the trash?"

"Fine," Rumper said, "but we're clearing the whole place next time. I still need the achievement."

"Make sure to step where I step. If you break the wrong tile, the alarm will sound."

This was something I was familiar with, recalling Merrill's training where I had to jump from one pillar to the next. I found following her steps simple. We jumped from one tile to the next, mindful to go one at a time to avoid crashing into one another. Rumper had the hardest time with it. I was pleased I found at least one thing I was better at than him.

The hallway continued in a spiral pattern, the walls arcing tighter and tighter until, after a few minutes of jumping, we reached the end. Entering a large chamber, I was amazed at how empty it was. Aside from coffins lining the walls and a large table in the middle, it was bare. I didn't see any sign of life.

"All right, Delmen, same as last time. Stay near me. Do whatever I tell you, understand?"

I nodded and raised my hammer, more at ease with fighting now. Citizens in this place weren't in their right mind. They forced me to kill in self-defense. I only hoped Meridia wasn't as mad as some of the others we had seen so far.

Rumper approached the table in the middle of the room.

Raising his sword, he struck the metal table with his blade. The ting of metal against metal echoed through the room. The only doors I spotted, one behind us and one on the opposite end, slammed shut.

"What have we here, Mr. Burke? Visitors?" I heard a man ask. The voice, followed by an insane cackle, came from everywhere.

"I don't know, Mr. Hare. Perhaps some weary travelers lost in the dark."

"I know! Let's show them our hospitality, shall we, Mr. Burke?"

"Why yes, Mr. Hare. Let's. It's been so long since anyone has seen our work. Let's show them our wonderful creations!"

Both of them laughed at the same time. The sound of their voices unnerved me. I found myself instinctively getting closer to Bunny for protection. Never in my life had I heard anyone talk like they did. This place was wrong.

When Burke and Hare began chanting in unison, chills went down my spine. I gripped my hammer tightly and prepared for what was coming.

9

"**W**elcome, friends, to Burke and Hare! Stick around. Don't go nowhere."

The floor shifted under us. Bunny pulled me away as the ground opened. A hole, twice the size of a human, was left where I had stood. From the hole, a creature started to emerge, elevated by a mechanical platform below it.

"Burke's the doctor! Hare's the sneak! You're our guests. Come on! Let's eat!"

I gagged when I saw the creature. It was an amalgamation of limbs belonging to multiple bodies, all functioning, with the head of a gnome. It snarled at us. Its dead eyes locked with mine for a moment. The monster raised his hands in the air, but instead of flesh and bone, a series of straps secured boulders to the stubs that were his arms. Every ounce of me wanted to run from the monstrosity.

"Meet our friend, the tailor gnome, with legs of sticks and hands of stone!" they chanted together.

The beast shouted and charged at Rumper, the closest to it. He raised his shield in time to deflect the boulders crashing down on him. The gnome-creature struck with such force I expected Rumper's shield to split in two but it held up. One quick swing of his sword later, the creature had a nasty looking gash across one of his arms. Black blood poured from the wound.

As the beast bellowed ferociously, the others swung into action, slinging spells and bullets and healing spells. I just stood there close to Bunny. Even if she didn't warn me to stay close, nothing in the world could make me attack the creature.

The beast suddenly pushed Rumper away. It bashed its stone fists into the floor over and over again. The room shook. My legs felt like rubber. Bunny grabbed my arm as red circles appeared on the floor, first a dozen, then nearly one hundred. We danced around the circles that covered more and more space on the floor until there were few places left to stand. She pulled me close to her in time for me to avoid falling boulders from above. Once they hit the ground, the rocks vanished. The four of them started all over again, Rumper drawing the beast's attention while the others battled it from afar.

This pattern cycled three more times, each time falling boulders becoming bigger and safe places to stand becoming harder to find. At last, the creature shrieked one last time, this one sounding less like a beast and more like a citizen in agony. It sank to the floor, dispatched, and crumbled to dust.

"Why Doctor Burke, they killed your friend!"

"It's okay, Mr. Hare. Let's try again!"

All the light in the room extinguished.

"What's happening?" I asked Bunny, still standing at my side. She slapped her hand over my mouth to silence me.

I heard a hiss of a fast-burning flame, and the room painted itself blood red. Fizzlestick, standing on the other side of the room, ignited a flare and tossed it in the center of the chamber. Being able to see by its light, I spotted faint outlines of dozens of creatures, skin the color of coal, as though every inch of their bodies were charred, even the whites of their eyes and the enamel on their teeth.

"Mr. Hare, our guests are tricky!"

Together, they both responded with a most sinister tone, "Dear minions, show them no pity!"

Bunny said one word to me before she raised her staff and cast a potent spell. "Stealth."

And I did. As she pushed me away from her, I crouched, finding my detection grid active, hugging my body. No amount of light in the room could reflect off my armor and reveal where I was. Shadows to hide in were too plentiful. I hugged the wall to avoid Bunny's spell, a fierce flame she set that encompassed half of the room with her at the center. The shadow creatures spotted her and charged. As they were about to strike, a bubble of white light surrounded her, channeled by Brunar. Her attackers, without weapons, scratched and clawed at the bubble while fire scorched their legs. They screamed like angry cats as they charged Bunny until, one by one, they hit the ground.

As the protective bubble surrounding Bunny flickered and faded away, so did her fire spell. With the last attacker dead, the lights in the room blazed once again.

"Mr. Hare, they killed your pets. Let us give them one last test!"

The metal table in the middle of the room split in two, as though lightning struck it, and the ground caved in. A platform rose, revealing an elf woman wearing a beautiful silk dress. My heart skipped a beat, thinking I found Meridia, preparing myself for the worst. But as she turned around to focus on us, I felt relief. It wasn't her.

Five more cracks of sound distracted me from her. The air practically buzzed with energy. I backed up until my back struck a pillar behind me. Looking around for the others, I saw them all hiding behind other posts, Bunny yelling at me to take cover. I couldn't hear her. I couldn't hear anything. As I spun around to get behind the pillar, I felt a jolt in my back. It sent me tumbling. Another jolt struck me. Each time, my red bar, my health, reduced considerably, then it stopped. My health replenished, presumably by Brunar's healing magic, and I could hear again.

Brunar rushed to my side, grabbed me by my collar, and dragged me behind my pillar. "Close your eyes, cover your ears, and stay out of the way!" he snapped at me before returning to the fight. I did as he said. I hated the elf. He was a spiteful bastard, but he didn't yet want me dead.

I squeezed my eyes shut, clapped my hands over my ears, and hid behind my pillar. Even when covering my ears, I could hear the cracks every so often and could see the health and mana bars of the others reduce, then rise again as they battled the elf woman. A few minutes later, I felt another tug on my collar. Opening my eyes, I saw Bunny and Brunar standing over me, both a few feet taller than I was, then I heard Dr. Burke and Mr. Hare. They sounded sad.

"Dr. Burke, they killed our friends."

"I know. It's time for them to leave, my friend."

Their voices faded. Gears ground together, and locks came undone. The door exiting the room slid open.

<<Light-armor rank 4>>
<<You have defeated Burke and Hare -- lvl 11>>
<<Reward: 9 guilders>>
<<Reward: Mr. Hare's Ring of Stealth. -10% reduction in detection ring.>>
<<Reward: Steamtown reputation +25>>
<<Level up! Open interface to select rewards.>>

I pulled the ring out of my inventory. It was a black onyx loop, sized for me, and contained an enchant I had never seen before. I slipped it on, pleased by the added stealth. The others stood at the exit waiting for me. I didn't have time to pause and choose my leveling rewards.

As I jogged across the room, they talked amongst themselves.

"Bunny, do you have time for Sawney Bean?" Rumper asked.

"Yeah, I suppose so."

"Good. Hopefully, we'll get the drop this time."

"Wait, we're going to skip Cleek Cave?" Fizzlestick asked.

"Yeah. I hate that boss. My rig has rendering issues in there. Too much water texturing," Rumper said. "If you want to do it, you need to find a tank with a better kit."

I had no idea what they were talking about. Remembering their earlier warnings, though, I kept my mouth shut. I followed them up a steep incline, steeper than any close in Steamtown.

A rancid stench grew more and more noticeable the higher we climbed. We reached a fork in the path where two wooden signs stuck out of the soft clay ground. One read "Bean Lair." The other read "Cleek Cave." Following the others to the left, away from the cave path, I felt anxious. It seemed we were approaching the end, and yet there was no sign of Meridia. I worried I would never find her, and wondered if Vasilia's information was accurate.

Bunny, noticing me behind her, slowed down and walked beside me. "Delmen, you've been very quiet."

"I don't know what to make of all this."

"What do you mean?"

"It's just that my life has changed so much in the last week. Before that, I did everything I could to reduce the amount of time I had to work with travelers. I didn't understand you all. I still don't. You talk like you're from another world, like none of this violence and death bothers you."

"Why would it bother us? If we die, we resurrect at the graveyard. So do you."

I sighed. "It's not that simple. You see my bounty. If I end up at the graveyard, guards will find me and send me to the stocks for mandate violation."

"You said that before. What are these mandates?" she asked.

"They're rules every citizen must follow. Breaking them sometimes means the difference between having a home and not having one. What I did was the worst violation of my mandates. I attacked a traveler. And the punishment for that is life in Steamtown Stockades."

Brunar, just ahead of us, heard everything I said. He stopped dead in his tracks and turned around. "Wait. You're telling me that you NPCs..." He paused. "Sorry. You citizens have rules that you must follow? Rules that you can break? I didn't know this game was so sophisticated."

"Our lives may be a game to you, but it's not a game to us!" I gripped my hammer, trying to suppress my urge to smack him.

Bunny placed her hand on my shoulder. The touch, a gentle one, calmed me down. "Hush, Brunar. He doesn't know. And nothing good can come from telling him."

"What don't I know?" I asked.

Bunny looked like she was going to tell me — like she was about to reveal a big secret, then she stopped. "Never mind. I hope you find Meridia. I hope you get your old life back."

The others ahead of us stopped. Rumper looked at Bunny with a smirk on his face. "Are you done with all this RP crap? Or do you want to break for tea?"

"Har har har," she said sarcastically. "Let's get this over with. If I don't sign off in the next twenty minutes, my wife won't be happy. It's my turn to cook dinner."

Rumper nodded and returned his attention to a door that appeared ahead of us. He pushed it open with his shield, and we slipped inside.

Where I had expected another horror show to await us, I

instead found a home, grander than any house I had seen, even the estate I robbed in High Mile. At the same time, it also stank to high heaven, like if you combined the fetid stench of every Steamtown close into one odor. I gagged a few times until I plugged my nose and breathed through my mouth. It didn't help much. I could taste the smell.

"What is that?" I asked Bunny.

"It's bad, isn't it? Like rotting onions and rancid meat mixed into one. I would say you get used to it, but you don't. Now as for what's coming up, you're not going to be happy. We have the entire Bean family to get through before we reach Sawney's lair. That means forty-seven non-stop attackers. Get your hammer out."

As I raised my weapon, Rumper clashed his sword into his shield. The sound bounced through the underground mansion, answered by harsh screams and calls to arms. One by one, a stream of men and women ran into what I could only describe as a sitting room. They all looked the same, with ratty auburn hair, camel-brown clothes, and sharp daggers as weapons. The nameplate above each indicated they were members of the Bean family, all around the same level. Each of them was as insane as the next. We battled them one or two at a time.

As we pushed our way through the sitting room and into the next cave, decorated with a decaying dining table stained by blood, they started to come at us from behind.

Bunny cast frost spells to freeze them in place. The closest attacker, a young woman, lashed out with her dagger after I struck her with my hammer. The blade sliced into my arm. While Brunar healed me, I deflected her next attack with my hammer, knocking the knife from her hand with such force it stuck into a nearby wall. I pulled my hammer back, swung it over my head, and smashed it into her skull.

She collapsed, dead, but another immediately took her place. I found myself being pressed back, trying my best to not trip over my own feet. My next attacker, a young man, lunged at me with his dagger. It caught on my guild armor and deflected, barely scratching the surface. Unable to recover from the attack, he fell at my feet, allowing me to dispatch him like I did his relative, with a few repeated hammer strikes. The battle dragged on. A chain of Bean corpses littered the ground behind us, some already starting to crumble to dust.

We fought our way into a kitchen. There I spotted citizens chained to the wall, although none were Meridia. As I approached them, they gnashed at me with their teeth, driven insane by their captors. I started to lose hope that Meridia would be herself if and when I found her.

Through the kitchen, we arrived at a sleeping area where dozens of piles of ratty rags littered the ground. More citizens were chained, some from the ceiling by their ankles, some to the floor, a tight collar strapped around their neck. Many were missing limbs. Some were passed out. They represented all races of citizens I have seen in Steamtown.

As I battled another one of Sawney Bean's children, or so I assumed, I wondered why the guards and why Governor Law tolerated these people living so close to the city, or living at all for that matter. I felt like I saw Eto for the very first time, and I didn't like the look of it. Residing in Steamtown was never easy, but knowing this kind of insanity and malice existed disheartened me.

We fought our way up a staircase, down a hallway, then up another staircase. Our attackers rushed out of rooms as we passed, never more than two or three at a time. At last, we reached what I assumed was the last room in the mansion. Ahead of us, two doors blocked our path secured by an iron padlock. While we continued to fight, Bunny worked on the lock.

As the last Bean child fell, I heard the thud of the padlock hitting the floor, and followed the group as they rushed into the room. The ceiling was twice as high as the rest of the mansion. A long table sat opposite a hearth on the first level of the room surrounded by dozens of half-broken chairs. Behind the table, a grand staircase led up to a balcony of sorts, that ended at a precipice. A cold gust of wind rushed through the cavern-like apartment. The damp wind chilled my bones.

Atop the stairs, I spotted Sawney Bean waiting for us. He wore nothing save a brown plaid kilt. Hundreds of scars stretched over his torso. Fury burned in his eyes. A tattered figure knelt on the floor beside him, and I gasped. It was her. It was Meridia. She wore the same dress she had on the last time I saw her, only now it was soaked in blood and stained by filth.

"Meridia," I whispered as I stepped forward. Bunny grabbed me by the arm and pulled me back, shaking her head. It was then that I noticed both Sawney Bean and Meridia's nametags, shining above their heads in blood-red letters.

"I'm sorry," Bunny said to me. "There's nothing we can do for her now. She's part of this place."

"What do you mean? We can subdue her and take her outside! I know once she's somewhere safe, she'll be herself again."

"No, Delmen. That's not how this world works. I'm even surprised I can have this conversation with you. You're different. It's as though you don't belong here."

"Enough! I have to try!"

Sawney Bean started to talk, but I raised my hammer and ran toward him. Doing so stopped his speech and sent him into a frenzy. He let go of a chain he held in his hand, the same chain leashing Meridia. She instantly reacted as well, freed from her captor, and looked up. Our eyes locked. For a moment, I felt like I recognized her and she recognized me. But the moment passed. She sped down the stairs like a vicious animal and lunged at me, sending me falling onto my back while she slashed me with her sharp fingernails.

I spotted Rumper's boots whirl by me as he hurried up the stairs and locked blades with Sawney. All I could do, though, was try to block Meridia's hands with my hammer. I couldn't bring myself to strike her.

With each swipe of her now bloody fingernails, my health bar reduced. She was unrelenting. I felt her nails dig into my flesh. The stinging attacks were still not enough to drive me to defend myself. She was my dearest friend in the world, the only real friend I had ever known. I loved her.

Her attacks ceased. I blinked a few times, unable to reconcile what had happened. A combination of a few fire spells left her clothes singed. And the black marks of where bullets embedded into her flesh appeared. She went limp and rolled off me, dead.

"No, no, no," I whimpered, sitting up so I could lift her into my arms. A sense of shock and disbelief surged through me. I looked at Bunny, seeing a few tears forming in her eyes. Then I spotted Fizzlestick who smiled as he fired on Sawney Bean. The rest of the battle was a blur. I hardly noticed the notifications appear in my field of vision.

<<One-handed rank 6>>
<<Light armor rank 5>>
<<You have defeated Sawney Bean -- lvl 14>>
<<Reward: 15 guilders>>
<<Reward: Sawney Bean's Charm - +10% incoming
   damage reduction>>
<<Reward: Steamtown reputation +50>>

I wept as Meridia's body started to crumble in my arms. "You didn't have to kill her," I mumbled to the others.

"We didn't have a choice. She was his vessel. As long as she lived, we couldn't kill the boss," Fizzlestick said. He sounded cocky, pleased with himself. He didn't seem to realize he was a cold-blooded murderer. He was without empathy as I sat in a disheveled mess on the ground, unhealed scratches still marked on my face.

I looked at Bunny, the only one who possessed some level of compassion, but she refused to look at me. She just said her goodbyes to her friends, asked them to escort me out, and then she froze in place.

I gulped after seeing her body become translucent, like a ghost. Then she vanished entirely. Her nameplate in my field of vision disappeared. Without her, I was left at the mercy of three heartless bastards.

"Which one of you is going to escort him out of here?" Rumper asked. They both scoffed at the idea and spoke amongst themselves.

Rumper mention signing off. He vanished a few moments later. The other two agreed to go to the Lothian Fields, an area I had heard about outside Steamtown. They each pulled out a flat, polished rock, and traced their fingers over a symbol on it. Fizzlestick ignored me completely, but Brunar smiled and winked. "This world isn't real. You aren't real. The only reason you exist is for our entertainment," he said before both of them vanished. About a minute later, their nameplates disappeared as well. I was alone.

> *<<Your group has been disbanded. You will be teleported to Steamtown Graveyard in 1 minute.>>*

I panicked. Echoes of Merrill's warnings and Vasilia's pleas echoed in my ears.

Did Merrill know this would happen? Has it happened before?

As I imagined my capture, I realized suddenly what the stockades were. They weren't just a prison. The stories were true. I would become like the citizens I battled here, meant to act as fodder for twisted and sadistic travelers to slaughter over and over and over again without mercy.

As the timer counted down, I stood up, wiped the tears from my cheeks, and readied my hammer, knowing full well if guards were waiting to apprehend me, I would fight. Then I would flee, and once free, I would tell the truth to as many people I could find willing to listen.

As the world faded to black, the graveyard started to appear. I knew what I had to do. I had to save myself, then rise against the governor, against the queen. I had to rid us of the injustices and lies travelers inflicted on us once and for all.

THE END

ABOUT THE AUTHOR

RJ Castiglione lives in Rhode Island with his husband (and best friend). During the day, he works in software technical support. At night and on the weekend, he writes stories that he enjoys imagining.

Check out his website at https://rjcastiglione.com for more, including information about how you can contribute to Steamtown Chronicles 2.

    facebook.com/rjcastiglione

    twitter.com/rjcasta

    amazon.com/author/rjcastiglione

    goodreads.com/rjcastiglione

ALSO BY RJ CASTIGLIONE

Liked this? You'll enjoy the Fjorgyn series, a healer-driven LitRPG series following Michael and his boyfriend, Clifford, as they work together to defeat the sinister Ankou Levent and the forces of the Elathian Empire.

https://books2read.com/u/bwY8OP

www.ingramcontent.com/pod-product-compliance
Lightning Source LLC
Chambersburg PA
CBHW032017180726
48283CB00008B/2715